Forest of the Dragon

Dragon Shifter Romance

Mac Flynn

All names, places, and events depicted in this book are fictional and products of the author's imagination.

No part of this publication may be reproduced, stored in a retrieval system, converted to another format, or transmitted in any form without explicit, written permission from the publisher of this work. For information regarding redistribution or to contact the author, write to the publisher at the following address.

Crescent Moon Studios, Inc.
P.O. Box 117
Riverside, WA 98849

Website: www.macflynn.com
Email: mac@macflynn.com

ISBN / EAN-13: 9781791814557

Copyright © 2018 by Mac Flynn

First Edition

CONTENTS

Chapter 1..1
Chapter 2..7
Chapter 3..13
Chapter 4..22
Chapter 5..29
Chapter 6..35
Chapter 7..44
Chapter 8..52
Chapter 9..60
Chapter 10..68
Chapter 11..76
Chapter 12..83
Chapter 13..90
Chapter 14..99
Chapter 15..107
Chapter 16..113
Chapter 17..119
Chapter 18..125
Chapter 19..131
Chapter 20..136
Chapter 21..143
Chapter 22..149

Chapter 23..156
Chapter 24..163
Chapter 25..169
Chapter 26..175

Continue the adventure.................................182
Other series by Mac Flynn............................189

FOREST OF THE DRAGON

CHAPTER 1

Cold. Cold and noisy.
That was my world at that moment as I stood leaning against the railing of the large balcony. At my back was the imperial castle of Xander Alexandros, lord of Alexandria. In front of me lay the frozen surface of Lake Beriadan. Ice covered every inch of its waters, and children laughed and yelped as they slipped across its surface.

Their voices were drowned out by the voices around me, and yet I was alone on the balcony. I grimaced and clapped my hands over my ears, but that did nothing to drown out the numerous voices. I threw my hands down to my sides and growled.

"That is a rather intimidating noise," a voice spoke up behind me.

I spun around and glared at the speaker. "Will you just shut-" I froze. Xander stood in the doorway that led into the castle. One of his eyebrows was arched. My shoulders drooped and I ran my hand through my hair. "Oh thank god, you're really there."

He frowned as he walked up to stand a foot before me. "Should I not be?"

I averted his curious gaze and shook my head. "No. I mean yes. Maybe?"

Xander cupped my chin in one hand and lifted my gaze to his. He smiled softly down at me and made my heart flutter. "What is the matter?"

I sighed. "Do you remember those voices I heard a few months ago? The ones Crates told us were the voices of the gods?" He nodded. "Well, I'm hearing them again."

He pursed his lips. "How long have they remained silent?"

I shrugged. "Ever since we defeated Phrixus two months ago."

"Are they the same as you heard before?" he wondered.

I winced. "That's the bad part. They sound louder. It's like there's a party in my head where I didn't invite any of them and they're all drunk."

"Can you understand what they are saying?" he asked me.

I drew my chin out of his grasp and wrapped my arms around myself as I shook my head. "Nope. It's just a bunch of murmurs, but I get the feeling from the tone of their voices that they think something's going to happen."

"Lord Xander!" On cue one of the castle sentries appeared in the doorway. He was low on breath, but still managed to stand at attention and salute his lord. "My Lord, a message has arrived from King Thorontur."

I furrowed my brow. "Who again?"

"The fae ruler of Viridi Silva, the forest to the northwest of my domain," Xander reminded me before he strode over to the guard. "What is the message?"

The guard shook his head. "The fae messenger would not-"

"Hey! Stop there!" came a shout from the hall behind the guard.

Xander strode into the passage with the guard and me close at his heels. We glanced down the left side of the hall and glimpsed a tall Arbor fae stride down the stone passage toward us. Behind him was an entourage of a half dozen castle guards who scampered after the dark-haired gentleman.

I glanced up at Xander. "I'm guessing it's Spiros's day off."

He nodded. "Unfortunately."

The young man stopped before Xander and bowed his head to the dragon lord. "It is a pleasure to see you again, Lord Xander."

The guards hurried up behind him and pointed their swords at the gentleman. The leader of the group glanced at Xander. "My Lord, he would not obey our orders-"

Xander smiled and waved his hand at the guard. "It is quite all right. You may return to your duties-" he glanced at the messenger, "-all of you. I will entertain our royal guest." The men bowed their heads and retreated.

I stepped up to Xander's side and squinted at the young man. He was about thirty with pointed ears and shimmering black hair. The man was as tall as Xander, but slim and with paler skin. His eyes were the greenish color of fresh moss on a tree trunk and his black hair fell down to his rear.

I pointed at him. "Don't we know you?"

"He is Durion, prince of the Arbor fae of Viridi Silva," Xander reminded me.

Durion smiled at me and bowed his head. "I have not forgotten your name, Maiden Miriam, nor the great deed you did for my people which can never be repaid."

I shook my head. "It's just Miriam, and don't mention it. It was more of a fluke than anything."

He lifted his gaze to mine and his eyes flashed with a brilliant green light. "I have heard of many other 'flukes' that have been attributed to your impressive powers as a Mare fae. Even to the ability to produce Soul Stones."

I shrugged. "More flukes."

"Prince Durion, please forgive me if I I sound rude, but what has brought you so urgently to my castle?" Xander spoke up.

Durion returned his attention to the dragon lord and pursed his lips. "Pardon my interest in your Maiden-" I cleared my throat, "-that is, in Miriam's abilities, but unfortunately they may be needed. You see, the humans have returned to Viridi Silva, and even now nestle themselves once more in the ruins of their ancient city, Pimeys."

Xander arched an eyebrow. "When did this occur?"

"The large group of humans were noticed traveling through the forest some three weeks ago. They have taken up residency in the ruins of the formerly cursed castle and we have seen them repairing parts of the fortification."

"Have you made any attempts to contact them?" Xander asked him.

Durion nodded. "Yes. Several messages have been left, once by night beside the largest of the tents and another by arrow pinned to the castle walls. They have not responded, and after each attempt at contact more work has been performed on the defenses."

Xander pursed his lips. "What does the king make of these humans and their actions?"

"My father-that is, King Thorontur believes they mean to take advantage of our smaller numbers and reclaim their lost territory," Durion told us.

Xander studied the young fae. "I sense you do not share your father's belief."

The prince straightened and pursed his lips. "I have observed them a great deal and can find no signs of aggression."

"Even in their rebuilding of the wall?" Xander wondered.

He nodded. "Yes. I would do the same if I were making a new home of an old one, and there is the people themselves. The men have brought their wives and children with them."

"So you favor a diplomatic route with them?" Xander persisted.

Durion stiffened a little more. "I cannot say for sure, Lord Xander, but it is on that front that my father wishes to see you-" his eyes flickered to me, "-both of you."

I pointed at myself. "Why me?"

"That is a matter on which he wishes to speak personally with you," Durion revealed as he glanced at Xander. "Will you come?"

Xander bowed his head. "We will come."

I glanced up at Xander and pursed my lips. "You think we should? I mean-" I tapped my temple, "-there's the voices problem."

He nodded. "An ally has asked for my aid. I must not forsake him."

I sighed and shrugged. "All right. When do we leave?"

"Immediately."

CHAPTER 2

"I do not like this idea," Darda muttered

My saddle jabbed into my rear and made me wince. "Neither do I."

It was several days later, and I now found myself atop a horse. Again. Beside me rode Darda, and in front of us was Xander and Durion on his own Arabian-esque steed. We were inside the Viridi Silva with its lush carpet of ferns and brush below us and the thick canopy of green leaves above us. The air was so thick I could have bottled it and named it Scent du Forest.

Xander turned his head to one side so that his eye fell on Darda. "It is a simple matter of diplomacy. We shall be back at the castle within a fortnight."

She shook her head. "We should not be without Spiros."

"His mind is preoccupied with his new bride, and I could not have left Alexandria in better hands," Xander reminded her.

Darda glanced over her shoulder at a hefty bag on the back of her horse and pursed her lips. "It is not Alexandria for which I am worried."

"You must believe me when I say my father would not have asked for your help were it not absolutely necessary," Durion apologized.

Xander smiled at him and shook his head. "There is no need to apologize. We are honored to be called by King Thorontur to aid your people."

A strong breeze blew over us, but provided no comfort against the muggy air. Rather, the heat from the wind made me gasp for air. I looked down at my heavy dress garb and frowned. "If Thorontur is going to want to see me *not* covered in sweat than I'm going to have to be a little more comfortable than this for the rest of the trip."

Darda's eyebrows crashed down. "That is the garb of a lady, Miriam, especially when riding."

"I'm going to be swimming in it soon if I don't slip into something more comfortable," I quipped as I focused on my clothes. My outfit was made from water so that at my whim the heavy dress changed to loose-fitting pants and an airy blouse-like shirt.

Durion reined in his horse and gaped at my changed appearance. "How were you able to do that?"

I sheepishly grinned. "Just a little water magic my mom showed me. She's the one I get my powers from."

"Then you can manipulate water without an exterior source that would bind to your magic?" he asked me.

I shrugged. "Yes?"

His eyes drifted over to Xander. "Your Maiden is an even greater fae than the stories have told."

FOREST OF THE DRAGON

Xander glanced at me and the twinkle in his eyes was better than any compliment. "She has certainly shown herself to be an outstanding woman in many ways."

Darda cleared her throat. "I would very much like to be in Metsan Keskella before nightfall so that I need not share my bed with any more bugs."

Durion studied me for a moment longer before he pointed his horse in the right direction. "We should reach the city before the noon hour."

We continued on our way, but I quickened the speed of my steed and sidled up beside Durion. I leaned forward and caught his eye. "So what powers do Arbor fae have?"

A bitter smile slipped onto his lips. "In days past I could have told you about the wonders we could create. There are tales of my people summoning huge swaths of forest to rise from the ground and cover hundreds of acres of bare ground in only a few seconds."

"So did they make the forest?" I asked him.

He swept his eyes over the canopy above our heads before he shook his head. "No. This forest is even more ancient than my people, though it was through our efforts that it grew to such borders."

"So why don't you do that anymore?" I wondered.

He stared ahead and pursed his lips. "After our battle with the humans those many years ago our power was diminished. We never recovered and can now hardly create enough growth to cover our own firewood needs." His eyes flickered to the far reaches of the forest. "Perhaps if we had been stronger than the citadel would have been cleansed far sooner, and we would not need to ask for your assistance in this matter."

I winced. "I'm sorry."

Durion looked to me and smiled as he shook his head. "It is none of your doing, sweet cousin, and I am glad for the opportunity to have met you, though I wish the circumstances of our meetings were different."

"How great in numbers are these humans?" Xander spoke up.

"It is as though the whole of Almukhafar has been emptied," he revealed. "All told I would be surprised if there were fewer than five hundred of the humans encamped in the ruins."

I arched an eyebrow. "Almukhafar? The outpost at the edge of the desert?"

Durion nodded. "The very same. When the humans were cast out of the forest the survivors were pushed south toward the desert. The thought was that no human could survive so close to such hot sands, but they surprised my people by surviving."

My mouth dropped open. "You guys tried to kill them?"

He closed his eyes and bowed his head. "It is not one of my people's finest hours."

"Have the humans attempted to make contact with your people?" Xander wondered.

Durion shook his head. "No. They have hardly left the grounds of the castle but to fetch wood and water. The humans have also brought a great deal of dried meat with them so that they-" He froze and yanked back on the reins of his horse. The steed stopped and he stood on his stirrups. "Something is amiss."

I swept my eyes over the area, but nothing moved. There was only the soft chirp of a bird from far away. "How can you tell?"

"There is a tension in the air transmitted through the soft breeze," he explained as he slipped off his horse. "I must see what is the matter."

"I will go with you," Xander offered as he, too, dismounted.

"Don't you dare leave me behind," I scolded him as I got off my horse.

"Nor I," Darda insisted.

FOREST OF THE DRAGON

Her joining us on the ground was interrupted by Xander thrusting his reins into her hands. "Someone must remain with the animals in case they should bolt." His eyes caught her gaze before they flickered to the pack behind her.

Darda pursed her lips, but bowed her head. "As you wish, My Lord." Durion wrapped his reins around a tree while I handed mine to Darda. She grasped my hand in hers and looked down into my eyes. "Be safe, dear Miriam."

I smiled up at her. "I'll be fine. I'm human, remember?"

"Would these humans say the same?" she countered. My smile fell off my face as I furrowed my brow.

"Miriam," Xander called from the edge of the path. Durion had already disappeared into the foliage.

"I'm coming!" I hissed.

I glanced back at Darda's worried face one last time before I slunk after my dragon lord. Together we hurried after our fae friend who slipped through the foliage like a green ghost. My eyes were on the uneven, grassy ground, but my mind was still back with Darda and her half-warning. I couldn't deny that I'd changed a lot since I landed in this strange world, but I was still me.

Right?

I stumbled over a half-rotten log and stretched out my hands so that I caught myself on the fall. A sharp bramble bush sliced a nice hole in one of my palms before I landed hard on my side. There was a sharp crack beneath me as my hip broke a fallen stick.

Durion, some thirty feet ahead of us, paused and turned to reveal his displeased expression. Xander helped me to my feet before he glanced at our friend and nodded. Durion returned the gesture and continued onward. I tried to follow him, but Xander held me back.

"You should go back," he whispered to me.

I looked up at him with a frown. "I'm fine. It's only a scratch."

His eyes studied me as he shook his head. "Something is bothering you. I can see it in your eyes."

I glanced past him at our disappearing guide. "Could we talk about this when we're not about to be left behind?"

Xander pursed his lips, but let us continue. Durion had slowed his pace some fifty yards up ahead and he stopped shortly after we reached him. A line of thick bushes blocked our way. Beyond them we could see two new Arbor fae hunched down beside Durion. The pair were covered head-to-foot in camouflage gear that allowed them to blend into the forest, and on their backs were bows. Their attention lay on something beyond the brush.

We reached them and knelt on the other side of Durion. His face was tense and his voice low as he nodded at the brush. "The humans have ventured farther than before."

I found a hole in the brambles and peeked through. Beyond the brush was a small glen, and in the bowl-shaped area crept a half dozen humans. Half the company was men, and the others were women. The youngest appeared to be a girl of eighteen with an honest face and a bit lower lip. All the humans had a quiver on their back, but few arrows to accompany the bows they held.

Durion glanced at one of the guards. "Have they found any prey?"

He nodded. "Yes, but the girl there-" he nodded at the young woman, "-frightened the deer and it ran away. They discussed turning back, but mentioned the low provisions and so continued onward."

The other fae guard leaned toward us. "If they continue much further they may see the city."

"Remain hidden unless they come within sight of the city. Then you may frighten them by making animal sounds," Durion instructed them. "I will inform my father of what has happened, and what you told me." He turned to us. "We must return to the horses immediately."

CHAPTER 3

We returned to the horses and found Darda with one of her daggers drawn and her face tense. "I thought you would never return," she commented as she handed us our reins. She raised her eyes to the canopy and frowned. "I have the feeling that we are not alone."

"That would be the Sentinels," Durion informed her as he mounted his horse.

Xander frowned. "So far from the city and during the daylight hours?"

"The explanations will have to wait for another time. We must hurry."

Durion turned his horse in the direction of the city and took off at a fast gallop. We hopped on our steeds and followed him as well as our inexperienced horses could follow the fae beast.

I sidled up to Xander and ducked a low branch before I leaned toward him. "What are the Sentinels?"

"Creatures conjured by the ancestors of the Arbor fae. They are dark copies of the fae who currently guard in the city, like shadows with their likeness."

I ate the branch of a bush, but spat out the leaves before I spoke. "How come I didn't see those things when we were last here?"

"They are not meant to be seen," Xander pointed out.

"And you didn't tell me about them why?"

"I did not inform you of their presence so as not to frighten you," he admitted.

Darda shuddered. "Such creatures as those gave me nightmares for a long time after my coming here for the first time."

Xander nodded. "They are rather a terrifying sight for those ignorant of their protective nature."

"So how come they didn't use these guards on the cursed castle?" I asked them.

"Their powers are limited. The farther they travel from the city the weaker they become so that any that would reach the castle would have been as helpless as a child," Xander explained.

"And they can do what with their full power?"

"They have the quickness of the fae upon which they are a copy, and the tenacity of an eselkatze."

I blinked at him. "A what again?"

"A donkey that resembles a cat," Darda told me. She stared ahead and pursed her lips. "They are the most persistent creatures I have met in either world."

Xander nodded. "Yes, and they know neither fear nor pity. Without the control of their fae and their creation purpose they would be a terrible force to behold."

I swept my eyes over the area and tightened my grip on the reins. "They sound nice."

"Fortunately, it is not they with whom we must speak," Xander reminded me as he hurried his horse forward.

FOREST OF THE DRAGON

After another hour of quick travel we reached the parting of the trees where stood the large, ancient tree of the Arbor fae. Its trunk could have fit a skyscraper, and its huge canopy reached as high as one. The branches were as thick as cars and the broad leaves unfurled to the size of umbrellas. The only change to the tree-dotted city was the city walls. They were finished, and dozens of guards walked their parapets with their eyes ever on the woods below them.

We traveled through the winding green streets and up to the castle that stood nestled against the high trunk. Servants took our steeds and Durion turned to us. "I know my father is eager to see you, but would you perhaps be in need of some rest?"

"Only a few minutes in order to wipe the dust of travel from our faces," Xander confirmed.

Durion nodded. "Then I will meet you there. I myself will inform my father of this turn in events."

Xander bowed his head. "We will be there shortly."

Durion hurried off, and a servant led us through the stone corridors to our rooms. Darda insisted on unpacking our things herself so that all three of us were in the room without curious eyes. It was only then, in the confines of the room, that she opened the thick leather satchel in which lay the box that contained the Theos Chime.

I stepped up behind her and looked over her shoulder. "I hope it survived the trip better than my rear."

A faint smile slipped onto her lips as she set the box on the bed and opened the lid. The glimmer of silver shone brightly in the dark box. "There is no need to worry. I once rode fifteen miles at a gallop over rough terrain with an egg safely tucked into my belt, and the shell was not even scuffed."

I blinked at her. "Why were you escorting an egg?"

"There is a festival of rebirth in the domain of Lord Cayden's people, and one of the races is such an egg race," she explained.

"So did you win?" I asked her.

She chuckled as she lifted the bell out. "Yes. There were two men who were faster than I, but their eggs were only fit to scramble."

The engraving on the bottom caught my attention. I leaned in close and squinted. "What was the last rhyme it said? The second one at the lakes?"

Xander walked over to us. "Two are joined by Mortal fate not even Death can separate."

I frowned. "It says something different now, but I still can't read it."

Xander looked over my shoulder and arched an eyebrow. "The language is now in an ancient form of fae."

"Can you read it?"

He cleared his throat and read the words aloud:

Within the cradle, slumbers thee, if one is able, come conquer me

I wrinkled my nose. "What the heck does that mean?"

Xander studied the message again and pursed his lips. "It means we may have stumbled on another god."

"So one of these humans might be a god?" I suggested.

He shook his head. "We cannot be sure, but the chime has warned us to remain on our guard."

"And to keep the chime close at all times," Darda added.

I leaned back and studied the box. "In a backpack?"

"No." She drew up her dress and revealed her undergarments. On the underside of the dress was a leather holster in which the box perfectly fit. She dropped her dress and there wasn't even a wrinkle. Darda smiled at me. "That, my dear Miriam, is why a dress is such an advantage."

FOREST OF THE DRAGON

I grinned. "Now if only it came with an air conditioner." I received a pair of blank looks before I shook my head. "Never mind. Now-" I swept my eyes over the room, "-where's a nice bowl of water to scrub myself clean."

The bowl lay on a nearby vanity. I was glad to dip my hands into the bowl of hot water and wash away the long miles of travel that clung to my skin. I raised my head and glanced at Xander who now stood by an open window. His gaze lay on the city below us. "Durion seemed pretty upset about the humans wandering around looking for food."

Xander didn't look at me as he gave a nod. "Yes. The fae are very possessive of their forest and its inhabitants."

I wiped my face dry and tossed the cloth aside before I walked over to Xander. "Before we get too deep into all this ownership stuff, could you tell me how King Thorontur rules over a forest that's supposed to be in your domain?"

"It is a rather old and precarious arrangement, one of which I was not well-acquainted until after our travels through there," he admitted as he studied the city. "My forefathers captured all the surrounding territory, but because of the combined army of humans and fae they could not take the forest."

I arched an eyebrow. "So the humans and fae fought together?"

He nodded. "Yes, though it was many thousands of years ago."

"So did they use magic against your ancestors?" I guessed.

"Yes, but the old records indicate they had a beast of immense strength that was capable of destroying three dragons by itself."

My eyebrows crashed down. "Wait, we're talking dragons like the dragons of today, or dragons like the dragons that could stay in dragon form practically forever?"

"The latter."

"Which one is that?"

"The dragons who could retain their beast form for as long as they wished."

"Ah. And the fae and humans had a beast that could destroy *three* of those by itself?"

"Yes."

"Oye. So the humans and fae had their falling out after they beat you dragons?"

"Yes. The ruins of the ancient city-I assume you recall them-"

I snorted. "How could I forget a place that tried to drain the life from everyone?"

"They were what remained of that human settlement. When my forefathers failed to capture the forest they made a truce to leave the woods to the fae in exchange for protecting the southern border from future intrusions, and the fae in turn made a truce with the humans so that they both were sentries. Many years later the humans and fae fell out over a disagreement of land and my forefathers took the side of the fae in the war. Those humans who were not destroyed fled to the desert, more specifically to Almukhafar."

I wrinkled my nose. "That small town at the edge of the desert?"

Xander smiled. "You remember it."

I grinned. "You're not the only one who's been giving themselves a refresher course."

Darda lifted her attention from our clothes and smiled at me. "She has been an eager student."

Xander bowed his head to our old friend. "I am grateful for your tutelage, and you are correct in your statement. The Outpost is where the survivors settled, and their descendants still inhabit the town."

"Or did until they decided to move back in," I added.

"Yes, and if you both are ready we will see if we cannot guarantee a smooth reintroduction, or at the very least a rocky truce," he suggested.

FOREST OF THE DRAGON

We took ourselves to the throne room of the most venerable Arbor fae king, Thorontur. His soft green robes were as immaculate as ever and his crown shone like the sun, but his face was worn by this new concern. At our coming, however, he rose to his feet and smiled at us. Beside the throne stood the heir-apparent, Durion.

Thorontur opened his arms to us. "A very warm greeting to my friends."

Xander knelt before him and bowed his head. "It is always a pleasure to help a kingdom such as what you rule, King Thorontur."

Thorontur's face fell a little. "I wish the occasion was a different one, but I fear this will not end well. My son tells me the humans have ventured farther than before."

Xander stood and faced the king. "By their own words they only ventured forth for food."

The king nodded. "That he also told me, but if the past has any lessons to teach us than it is that humans grasp more than what is theirs. Then, they might have spoken those words for you to overhear and thus lull us into a false reasoning."

Durion pursed his lips. "My men are more than capable of avoiding their sight-"

"-but can you guarantee they would not be seen by their desert casters?" Thorontur countered.

I arched an eyebrow. "A what?"

Thorontur turned his attention to me. "Humans are very adept at harnessing the magic inherent in elements, though not as much as we fae. This particular group of humans has brought with them others that are capable of controlling the winds, a unique ability that unfortunately the fae no longer possess and may not have much ability to fight against considering our weaker abilities since our fight against them so many thousands of years ago."

Xander stiffened. "If the only option you see is war than I am afraid I cannot allow my people nor myself to become involved."

The king shook his head. "Nor would I wish such an outcome. I have invited you both here to appoint you as arbitrators in the dealings between the humans and we fae."

"What terms of yours would we pass to the humans?" Xander asked him.

Thorontur sat down on his throne and cleared his throat. "Naturally, we would wish to retain as much control over the forest as was hard-fought so many years ago, but we will not be greedy. They may have their old city of Pimeys-provided they do not build a wall around their perimeters-and a few dozen acres around which to live and grow their food."

"Father, that would hardly sustain as large a group as has come," Durion protested.

His father whipped his head to him and frowned. "We have discussed this before, my son. If the humans have brought too many of their kind with them then they must return to the Outpost until such time as they can prove their commitment to peace."

"And that would be when?" I spoke up.

Thorontur leaned back against the rear of his throne and furrowed his brow. "Perhaps a few hundred years."

My mouth dropped open. "But they'll all be dead by then!"

"Then their children will be the inheritors of their goodness," he commented.

"If they are to be confined to such a space for their living, what of their hunting?" Xander reminded him.

"They would be confined to the same area until a future treaty decides those borders," Thorontur revealed.

I frowned. "But those are stupid-" A heavy hand fell on my shoulder. I looked behind me and found myself staring into Darda's stern gaze. She shook her head. My eyebrows crashed down, but I held my tongue.

"Are there any other terms or messages you wish to be passed along?" Xander asked him.

Thorontur shook his head. "No, that should suffice for a rough treaty."

"And the time in which they must reply?"

"Three days."

Xander bowed his head. "We will pass your terms on to the leaders of the humans."

The king smiled. "I am much relieved by your willingness to help us in our hour of need. Now, what do you say to some refreshments before you venture into the other camp?"

Xander's eyes flickered to my frowning face before he shook his head. "I hope to drink soon at the table of diplomacy, but to do that we must carry your terms to the humans. We will return in short time with their reply."

Durion stepped forward. "I will take you to them."

CHAPTER 4

We left the throne room and made our way through the halls to the stables. Xander walked even with Durion and glanced over at our fae friend. "How firm is your father with these terms?"

A bitter smile slipped onto Durion's lips. "You are kind to use the word 'terms,' but I fear the humans will see them more as demands."

"If these humans are like we normally are than he's trying to fit a square box into a round hole," I quipped.

Durion glanced over his shoulder and nodded. "That is what I fear." He stared ahead and sighed. "I know he means well for our people, but we would not tolerate such conditions."

"What terms would you request?" Xander asked him.

Durion shook his head. "It is not my place to question my father's decisions. I am entrusted with carrying them through to the letter, and I will do so regardless of what is asked of me."

"Have you observed these humans?" my dragon lord wondered.

Our guide nodded. "Yes, but there is little I can tell you other than they appear to be afflicted with an uncomfortable disease."

My blood ran cold. "Disease? What kind of disease?"

Durion chuckled. "From what we overheard from the human physicians, the desert people are unaccustomed to the damp air and have developed nausea from the humidity. That has forced the women and children to take up the duties of the men, as you witnessed from the inexperienced woman in the hunting group."

"How great a number is ill?" Darda spoke up.

"A good half, so you see the greater peril in my father's terms," he mused as we reached the stables on the lowest floor of the castle. He climbed onto his steed as we did ours. Darda had some difficulty with her package, but managed to sit side-saddle. Durion turned his steed toward us. "It would be as though we were presenting a wounded werewolf with wolf's bane."

"Then we will have to make the pill as easy to swallow as possible," Xander returned.

Durion pursed his lips and directed his horse toward the stable doors. "For all our sakes, I hope you will succeed."

We trotted through the root-bound city and out into the thick forest. As our group approached the location of the citadel Xander sidled up beside my horse and caught my eyes. "It may be wise to keep your fae powers hidden, or at least suppressed."

I frowned at him. "You, too?"

He arched an eyebrow. "Pardon?"

I jerked my thumb over my shoulder at my shadow, Darda. "She already said something about me being a fae making a difference. I'm still human. I mean-" I gestured to the green-toned skin of Durion, "-I look more human than any fae."

Xander pursed his lips as he studied me. "You take personal offense at our suggestions."

"When you're talking about me not being human I tend to take that as a personal comment," I quipped.

"Unfortunately, any conflict of interest may ruin our initial standing with the humans," he pointed out.

I tightened my grip on the reins and pursed my lips. "Fine, but if shit hits the fans I'm going to use everything I've got to get us out of there, all right?"

Xander's eyes twinkled at me as he chuckled. "Your euphemisms never cease to amaze me."

Darda wrinkled her nose. "I would much prefer they be a little cleaner, especially in front of strangers."

I furrowed my brow and glanced at Durion's back. "Who *is* in charge of these humans?"

He turned his head to one side so one of his eyes fell on us. "They refer to their leader as 'lord,' but also listen to the wisdom meted out by the class of desert casters of which my father spoke."

"What kind of damage can they do with their wind?" I asked him.

He shook his head. "We are not sure. At the edge of the desert they can command the wind to create dust storms that protected Almukhafar from bands of thieves and stampeding naqia. Within the confines of the forest we cannot guess what their winds may do to the trees and grass."

"Is this lord a reasonable man?" Xander wondered.

Durion pursed his lips. "He is a better leader when his daughter is present. She appears to be a calming force for his natural tendency to anger and a great comfort to her people."

"Has any other effort been made to contact them other than through writing?" Xander continued.

FOREST OF THE DRAGON

"No. We did not wish for our numbers to be known, so we have remained out of sight."

"How have you planned for us to approach them?"

Durion nodded in the direction ahead of us. "Two of my men await us near the human camp. They will be our escort and we will make contact with their own sentries. Hopefully a small show of force will avoid our being placed in the dungeon of the keep before we receive an interview with the lord."

We continued on for a half a mile before Durion stopped and whistled like a sweet song bird. Nothing happened. He frowned and whistled again. The result was the same. "Something has happened to my men."

Darda stiffened and her eyes flickered over the area. "We are being-"

A dozen people leapt out of the bushes and surrounded us. They held primitive spears and bows, but the quantity made up for the quality. The people were a mix of men and women, and they all wore thin shirts with cutoff pants. Some of them noticeably shivered beneath the cool shadows of the trees.

One of the men, a gentleman of about forty with short, sandy hair and a stern face, stepped forward so that he stood in front of us. "Get off your horses and come with us peacefully, and no one will get hurt."

Durion clenched his reins as he frowned at the human. "Where are my men?"

"Safe, and you'll see them soon when you come with us," the man assured him.

Xander stood in his stirrups so that he towered over the rest of us. "I am Lord Xander Alexandros of Alexandria. My friends and I have come to meet with your lord to broker a peace."

The human looked to Durion and scoffed. "Come to spy on us, more likely."

"With horses and a couple of women?" I quipped.

The man glared at me. "A woman can be as dangerous as any man, now get off your horses and come with me."

Durion glanced at Xander who gave a nod. We dismounted and our steeds were taken from us. At the passing of the reins of Durion's horse, however, the animal reared up. Its front hooves pawed the air and forced its human handlers to dive out of the way. Once free the horse turned tail and raced into the woods. In a few seconds she was gone.

The human leader turned to us and arched an eyebrow. "Your fae horses don't seem to be that loyal."

Durion smiled. "On the contrary, without their rider they are trained to return to the stables. Soon my people will know I am missing and go in search of me."

The man arched an eyebrow. "All that fuss for a scout? And that was a mighty fine steed for a soldier to be given."

Durion stood tall. "All of our steeds are fine."

"Maybe," the human replied. He studied Durion a little longer before he jerked his head in the direction of the keep. "Let's go."

We were marched on foot in a block formation with the humans around us. Xander walked beside Durion, and Darda and I were march-mates. The distance to the ruined castle once inhabited by the ancestors of the humans was only a hundred yards off. The trees parted as they had before, but instead of an empty field there was a large encampment of tents. There were so many that they were wall-to-wall leather and canvas with narrow paths between them and intersecting alleys that ran parallel to those like a giant tic-tac-toe board. Children played tag along the paths and women gossiped around open fires placed at the wider intersections. I saw few men above the age of sixteen among the tents.

FOREST OF THE DRAGON

A large tent stood on the left ad stretched for a hundred feet. One of the narrow sides faced us and the flap was open to reveal the long interior. Beds lined both walls, and nearly all of them were occupied by adults. Those were the people struck down by the vastly different environment of the forest compared to the desert. Women who hardly looked in better health than them soothed their aching bodies with broth and damp rags on their foreheads.

Xander leaned toward Durion and lowered his voice to a whisper I barely overheard. "Have there always been this many humans here?"

Durion shook his head. "No. More have come since I was last here."

"Quiet!" the human leader barked.

We were directed around the open edge of the camp and toward the keep. One of the men hurried ahead, and in a minute we followed through the ruined arches. Some of the ramparts and walls had been puddied and patched, but the supplies now lay abandoned in a corner, their owners no doubt stricken by the illness.

We were led to the open-air throne room. That area, too, had its share of humans, about two dozen in number. Some were thinly garbed guards, but twenty of those present were robed people who stood along the ruined walls on either side of us. Their clothes were tan colored and had large, airy hoods which at the present lay on their backs. They had their backs to the ruined walls and stared straight ahead like sentinels. At the back of the long room stood a taller robed man of about fifty with a long brown beard. At his side was the young woman from the hunting party. She held a heavy leather tome in her hands and bit her lower lip as we approached the throne.

The stone seat was worn down by countless centuries of neglect, but seated comfortably within its large dimensions was a human of immense size. Like the other humans his hair was sandy, a color caused by their naturally dark strands being bleached by the desert sun. He wore a light shirt and pants, but over his shoulders lay a thick skin

He swept his dark brown eyes over us and smiled. "So the trap has caught a valuable mouse."

CHAPTER 5

We were stopped before him and Xander arched an eyebrow. "A trap?"

The man nodded. "Yes. Once the fae spies were detained we realized others might replace them, so I had some of my men wait around for that change."

"Where are the other scouts?" Durion asked him.

Our host turned his attention to Durion and arched an eyebrow. "You have it a little backwards. My men only captured spies, and terrible ones at that for a child defeated their hiding."

The lord gestured to a young man who stood at his side opposite that of the tall robed man. The man was about twenty-five with long blond hair tied back in a tail over his back and a pair of green eyes that made me gasp. His skin wasn't as dark as those in the camp, but he wore their thin clothing over his thin but lithe body.

"This lad here, a new arrival from our old home, is-as he puts it-a master at hide-and-go-seek. He found your men within a few minutes of being posted near their position," the lord informed us. A serving girl hurried past our group with a tray and a single large mug in hand. She passed the drink to the man upon the throne who raised it to his guard. "To you, Sala, and may you find more rats."

The young man smiled and bowed his head. "I'm glad to have some entertainment, Lord Herra."

A stifled laugh escaped Durion's throat. The lord of the humans whipped his head to him and frowned. "Why are you laughing? That was the title given to my ancestors by the fae when they ruled over this area."

Durion suppressed his smile and shook his head. "The word 'herra' means 'lord.'"

I snorted. "So he's calling himself 'Lord Lord?'"

"Miriam. . ." Darda scolded me.

A dark shadow slipped onto the lord's expression as he looked up at the robed man at his other side. "You informed me that was the proper name."

The man's face turned ashen and he furiously bowed his head. I wondered if his head was going to go flying off like a broken bobble doll. "My apologies, my lord. My assistant made a mistake." His meek demeanor turned to ire as he looked to the young woman at his side. "Look up the name again!" he snapped at her.

She shrank beneath his anger. "But I told you, the name was-"

"Don't talk back to me! Just look it up!" he growled.

The girl opened the book and furiously flipped through the pages until she reached the middle. Her finger traveled down the pages for a few moments before the robed man snatched the book from her and looked it over himself. His eyes widened and a smile brightened his face as he looked down at the human lord. "My lord, your title is 'Lord Mies.'"

"And that means what?" Lord Mies snapped.

"Lord of Men," the robed man explained.

The newly named lord glanced at Durion. "Is that true?"

Durion nodded. "It is."

Lord Mies settled into his seat and pursed his lips as he studied us. "You'll have to forgive the slip-up." His eyes flickered to Durion. "It's been a long time since the Great Exile and my people have lost a lot of our heritage."

Xander stepped forward and knelt on one knee before the lord. "Lord Mies, my name is Xander-"

"I've already been informed of your coming," Lord Mies interrupted as he studied my dragon lord with a frown. "I've heard your name spoken of with respect, lord of dragons, so you can imagine that I'm a little surprised to find you here."

Xander lifted his head and furrowed his brow. "Why is that?"

He took a swig of his drink that left a frothy beard on his attached beard. "You demean yourself by being under the thumb of the fae king. Why should I or anyone talk to a diplomat who's nothing more than a puppet for my enemy?"

Xander stood and shook his head. "I am under no person's thumb, fae or human. Like you, the welfare of my people is my chief concern, and a war on my southern border would certain endanger that welfare."

Mies scoffed, but he leaned back in his throne and his face softened. "Then what do you want to say to me?"

"King Thorontur offers you your old fortress along with several dozen acres that surround its perimeters," Xander revealed.

His eyebrows crashed down. "That's it? What does his highness expect us to do, starve?"

"His suggestion was for some of your people to return to Almukhafar," Xander told him.

Mies gestured to the area around us. "Which would you rather prefer: the lush, cool green of this ancient forest or the hot, bitter emptiness of the desert?"

"I would want what is best for my people," Xander replied.

He returned his attention to Xander and arched an eyebrow. "A good answer, probably the best you could give me, but that doesn't solve this problem. If we can't farm then would we be allowed to hunt?"

"During later negotiations that might be an option," Xander told him.

A bitter laugh escaped his lips. "Would that be before or after starvation forced us back to that terrible desert?" Xander opened his mouth, but Mies held up his hand and shook his head. "No, dragon lord. You can go back to that high lord of the cursed fae-" Durion stiffened, but kept his mouth closed, "-and tell him that those aren't terms. They're a death sentence for us. That desert-" he pointed in the direction of the oasis, "-is slowly killing our old customs, and now that we have a chance to take back what's ours I won't let my people fade into that dry land just because he's afraid of a little competition in the forest."

"And that is your final message to King Thorontur?" Xander asked him.

"Word-for-word, if you can remember all of it," Mies confirmed as he stood. He patted his belly and belched. "Now then, there's no hard feelings on my part, so you're welcome to stay for lunch. There isn't much, but we've done what we could."

Durion stepped forward. "I would like my men-my fellow sentries to be released."

A sly grin slipped onto Mies's lips as he studied our fae friend. "Your men, are they? You must be pretty high up in your circles to not only have men under your command but to be escorting these emissaries-" he nodded at we three, "-into my domain."

FOREST OF THE DRAGON

Durion stood tall and firm. "Whatever rank I possess, I would still like those fae released."

Mies shook his head. "I can't do that. They're my only guarantee that your king won't do anything stupid to my people."

Durion's eyebrows crashed down and he took a step forward, but Xander caught him. The fae pulled against him and toward the throne. "But they have done nothing to warrant being held against their will!"

"Spying is something, and leaving threatening notes," Mies countered.

"Those notes were a welcome to you!" Durion argued.

Mies scoffed. "Do you expect me to believe that notes left in the dead of night are not threatening?"

Xander continued to contain Durion as he looked up at the human. "My Lord, I am sure if you would read the contents they would prove this young fae's words."

Mies shook his head. "We can't read them."

"But they are written in your ancient tongue!" Durion insisted.

Mies sneered at him. "Most of our literate class was wiped out in the war and that knowledge was lost within a few generations. These books-" he gestured to the tome once more held by the girl, "-are all that remains of our ability to write, and even they're a mess of the dragon tongue of the desert and our own vague memories of our former writing skill."

"If I am given some time with these notes I might be able to decipher them for you," Xander offered.

The human lord shook his head. "I can't accept your interpretation, dragon lord. If there was someone outside of your group I could trust then I would, but as things stand I won't release the spies."

A great din arose behind us, and all the company turned in that direction. Dogs barked and children laughed down the camp, but the noise grew louder as it approached our position. The din paused and a few moments later a thinly clothed man with a long spear hurried into the ruined throne room and stopped before the stone seat. He gasped for air as he bowed his head to his lord. "My. . .my lord-" he wheezed as he looked up at Mies, "-*he* is here."

Mies arched an eyebrow. "Has he brought what we asked?"

The guard nodded. "Yes, and then some. A whole train of eselkatze loaded with everything we could ever need."

A smile slipped onto Mies's lips. "Then let him in. By all means, let him in and see if he doesn't want to be our emissary in this farce of diplomacy."

The guard nodded and hurried off to obey. The cheerful sounds grew closer again as I glanced at Xander. He was tense, but there was a curious light in his eyes. That light grew as a great herd of people strode into the throne room. The group was made up mostly of children with a few stray animals thrown into the mix. At the head of the odd parade was a very familiar, and snout-nosed, face.

Tillit paused just short of where we stood and smiled at each of us in our turn. "I wondered how long it would take you guys to get into this mess."

CHAPTER 6

Xander returned the smile and bowed his head. "And a warm greeting to you, my sus friend."

Mies frowned as he glanced between the dragon and the sus. "You two know each other?"

Tillit didn't move his gaze from Xander as he nodded. "Yes, my lord, very well. Lord Xander and his Maiden Miriam are two of the best people I've ever known, but she-" his eyes flickered to Darda and his smile changed to mischievous, "-she's someone you have to watch out for."

Darda glared back at him. "You, Tillit, are a swine and a liar."

Tillit chuckled as he bowed his head to her. "I take those both as a compliment, but the second one only when it's for the common good."

"Will you vouch for their honesty?" Mies spoke up.

Tillit walked past us and up to Mies where he winked at the lord. "There's no one I'd trust more in a pinch, though I wish they'd stop getting me into them."

"You invited yourself into this one," Xander pointed out.

Tillit turned to Xander and held up his hands in front of himself. "Not Tillit, My Lord. I only come as an angel of food for these starving people."

"And into the middle of a war zone," I quipped.

Durion stepped forward close to Tillit and caught his gaze. "Tillit, please convince Lord Mies that my men are not a threat to his people, and that by holding them as tools he does himself no favors."

Mies frowned at him. "Not without those notes being read."

Tillit glanced between the bickering men. "What notes?"

"My people left several notes of welcome to Lord Mies and his people, but he believes they are threats," Durion explained.

Tillit laughed. "Threats from old Thorontur? Maybe, but he has the tenacity to say it to his foe's face."

"That has yet to be proven, and we have no third party who is able to read them," Mies argued.

Tillit hitched up his pants and grinned at Mies. "I'll read them for you."

Mies arched an eyebrow at the sus. "You can read?"

Tillit's face fell along with his ample stomach. "Why does no one believe that Tillit can read?"

Durion glanced at our 'host.' "Will you take Tillit's word if he communicates the contents of the notes?"

The lord stroked his beard for a moment before he nodded. "Yes, so long as he can read the ancient text."

Tillit straightened and held his head up high. "Bring the notes! Tillit can read any language in the world!"

FOREST OF THE DRAGON

Mies nodded at one of his guards. The man disappeared for a moment into the ruins before he returned, this time bearing a small bundle of paper. He handed them to Tillit who unfolded the top note and scanned the page.

Mies's eyes flickered between the paper and the sus's tense face. "Well? Have you learned anything from it?"

Tillit nodded. "Yes. Tillit has learned that his eyes are not as clear as they used to be." He glanced at Durion. "Must you fae have such beautiful, scrawling, *tiny* handwriting?"

Durion sheepishly shrugged. "The king insisted on writing them all himself."

"What do they say?" Mies persisted.

Tillit returned his attention to the paper and cleared his throat. "This one says that the fae would like to speak to the leader of the humans to set up conditions of occupation." He leaned forward and squinted. "There's also something about a dinner within a fortnight in honor of the leader and his guards."

"That letter was written three weeks ago," Durion added.

Tillit chuckled as he folded the note. "Well, there's always a chance to reschedule."

Durion turned to Mies who's brow was furrowed. "Will you now free my men?"

Mies glanced over to our fae friend and pursed his lips before he gave a curt nod. "I will, but only if you take their place."

Durion started back, and Xander stepped forward. "My Lord, you do not know of what you ask!"

"Then enlighten me or agree to my terms," Mies snapped.

"Father!" The company turned to the right of the hall where an archway still stood. Beneath the stone arch stood a beautiful young woman of twenty. Her long brown hair cascaded over her shoulders in humidity-created ringlets and her skin was as far as the desert sands after a gentle breeze. However, she stalked into the throne room with the grace of an angered elephant and marched up to the human lord. She put her hands on her thin hips and glared up at the taller man. "Is that any way to treat our guests?"

Mies took a step back away from her and winced beneath her heated gaze. "Now is not the time, my little naqia-"

"Now is the *only* time, Father, as you well know from your rounds through the tent," she snapped. He cringed as she turned to us. Her ire fell and was replaced by a bright smile. She clasped her hands in front of her and bowed low to us. "I welcome you, our honored guests, to this ancient abode of our ancestors, and hope your journey was not too fraught with danger."

Xander smiled and returned the bow. "On behalf of our company I thank you, and am very eager to know with whom we speak."

The young woman raised her head and her smile widened. "I am Valo, daughter of the lord of humans."

"An admirable name for such a beautiful young woman," Xander complimented her.

"Valo," a voice whispered close beside me.

I glanced over our group and my gaze fell on Durion. Our fae friend's jaw was slightly ajar as he gaped at the beautiful young human. I had to stifle a a snort of bemusement at his love-struck expression. Darda stood close beside me, and her eyes flickered to mine and she barely shook her head, but there was a mischievous look in her own gaze.

"Valo, please remove yourself from the throne room," her father commanded as he stabbed a finger in the direction of the archway. "We're talking about important matters that you can't-" a fiery look from his daughter made him pause before he cleared his throat, "-that you might not understand."

FOREST OF THE DRAGON

She grasped his hands in hers and looked into his eyes. "I understand the suffering of our people as you do, Father, but we can't trap others to protect them. They wouldn't wish for us to protect them in such a way."

Mies pursed his lips, but sighed and hung his head. "You're right, my little naqia. We can't stoop to their level." Valo rolled her eyes, but her father missed the gesture as he turned to Durion. "You may have your men back. I will instruct my men to return them to the edge of the woods, but see that they do not approach that close to our camp again."

Durion stepped up to the lord and bowed. "With your permission, I would like to see your sick. My men and I may be of some help in healing their ills."

Valo smiled down at him. "That is very kind of you."

The young fae lifted his eyes to her and he seemed to turn into a bundle of tightly wound nerves. "I thank you, Lady Kaunis-that is, Lady Valo. My men thank you as well, and I thank you."

Valo laughed, and the sound was like wind chimes in a gentle breeze. I was a little jealous. "You are a funny knight, sir-"

"Durion," he informed her.

"Sir Durion, then," she finished with her sparkling smile.

Mies belched and broke the magic between the pair. "If you're done here then go to the tent. Sala here-" he gestured to the young man who stood at the side of the throne, "-can show you the way, and release your men for you."

Durion bowed his head to the lord. "Thank you, Lord Mies."

Mies scoffed. "Don't thank me yet. I still won't agree to those outlandish terms of your king, and that-" his eyes flickered to Xander, "-is still the message I want sent back to him."

"I will relay it," Xander swore.

"Good, now-" he wrapped one arm across Xander's shoulders and turned them so they stood side-by-side, "-let's go eat." Mies led Xander out of the throne room via the same side arch through which Valo had entered.

Durion was reluctantly led away by the smiling youth, leaving Darda and me with the addition of Tillit. The sus patted his own ample stomach and grinned. "Some food after that trip would do a sus wonders." He followed the pair through the archway.

I lost my appetite at the thought of watching the drink-frothed man eat, so I turned to his daughter. "Is there any way I can look around?"

She nodded. "Of course. I'm sure we can find a guide for you-"

"I have such a creature," a voice spoke up, and I found myself turning to the throne room. The tan-robed priest strode over to us with the tome in hand and the young woman scurrying behind him. He stopped before us and gestured to his young charge. "Mufid here has time to show you the encampment."

I looked past him at the meek young woman. Her head was bowed and she clasped her hands one on top of the other against the front-center of her chest. "Thanks, but I'm sure we can find our way around."

"Ours is a small community, and it would ease the people's apprehension about seeing strangers if you were to be accompanied by a familiar face," he pointed out. "And Mufid-" he half-turned to the young woman and looked down at her with a stern expression, "-is eager to show you the encampment, are you not?"

She bowed her head lower and nearly lost her balance. "I-I would be honored to be your guide."

"And we would be honored to have you accompany us," Darda spoke up with a soft smile. Mufid raised her eyes high enough to see the gentle gesture and a ghost of a smile slipped onto her own lips.

The priest gave a curt nod. "Then I will leave you to her. Good day." He strode off, taking with him the other robed individuals as they left in a long, solemn train of two abreast.

Valo bowed low to us. "I, too, must go. My father will expect me to be by his side." She hurried off, leaving us with our nervous guide.

I glanced at Darda and jerked my head at where Valo had gone. "Do you think he needs her more than she needs to be around?"

Darda wagged a finger at me. "Politics of state is no place for a woman's mind to wander."

"Tell that to this group," I quipped as my gaze fell on our young escort. Her head was still bowed and one toe had began to bury itself into the dirt floor. I imagined the rest of her would follow if I didn't put a stop to things. "So your name's Muffy, right?"

"Mufid," she corrected me.

"What's it mean?"

"In the ancient language of Almukhafar it means 'useful,'" she explained.

I arched an eyebrow. "That's a-well, a very descriptive name."

"A very *nice* name," Darda emphasized.

Mufid bit her lower lip. "It was given to me by Father Darbat Qawia."

I blinked at her. "Who?"

"He's the gentleman who just left, the most exalted priest of the desert casters, and my guardian," she told me.

I winced. "Lucky you."

"Miriam," Darda scolded me.

"The casters adopted me when I was very young. My-" she bit her lip and clutched one hand against the center of her chest, "-my parents were killed by raiders when I was five. My mother hid me in a basket to save me, and after everyone had gone a group of priests passed by and took me with them. As a ward of the temple I was given a name and the task to learn the books."

I snorted. "You mean so he wouldn't have to read them?"

"Father Darbat-well, he respects knowledge, but he doesn't often consult the books himself," she admitted.

A sly grin slipped onto my lips. "So what you're saying is he likes knowledge, he just doesn't use it himself."

She couldn't hide the small smile that teased the corners of her lips. "That. . .that's one way to say it."

"So does he often loan you out as a guide?" I wondered.

She winced and averted her eyes from us as she bit her lower lip. "To be truthful I've never had this honor, but-well, you see-"

"You need not hesitate to speak plainly before us," Darda soothed her.

Mufid's eyes flickered up to me. "To be truthful he's very interested in you."

I arched an eyebrow. "Why me?"

"As a wind user he can sense the natural energy around people, and even fae," she explained as she tilted her head to one side and studied me. "He senses a lot of that energy around you, and wanted me to ask if you have any elemental gifts."

I winced. "Oh, um, well, I don't know about elemental-"

"Miriam is merely very attuned to the natural elements, but has no abilities herself," Darda spoke up.

I slipped my arm over her shoulders which made her jump and whip her head up to me. "I'm also very attuned to having a good time, so how about we go on that tour now, Muffy?"

FOREST OF THE DRAGON

"My name if Mufid," she corrected me.

"I prefer my nickname for you, my dear Muffy." I walked forward and took the staggering young girl with me. "Now let's go see the sights."

CHAPTER 7

We strode out of the ruins and into the fresh, bright air of the open field. The smoke from camp fires rose into the air and signaled the lunch hour. Throngs of people stood in long lines up and down the tent city with bowls in their hands and hunger in their eyes. At the head of every line, at some ten different points in the makeshift city, were cooking fires where women ladled a thick brothy soup into their bowls.

At the far end of the camp stood a long train of what some a dozen creatures that I guessed were eselkatze. They looked like mules, but their ears were shaped like those of a cat and their eyes had slits. Their long tails were like whips with their hair braided around a thick stalk of flesh and bone. The creatures were staked to the ground via their halters and they munched away on the grass as their backs, laden with heavy packs, were unloaded by many men. I caught sight of grain bags and pouches of dried meats, food courtesy of Tillit's efforts.

I nodded at the unloading. "Did Tillit bring all that?"

Muffy nodded. "Yes. Master Tillit was very kind to bring us provisions from our old home."

"For a profit. . ." Darda muttered.

Muffy looked aghast at her as she shook her head. "Oh no! Master Tillit was very generous with his prices! We couldn't have expected half the food through any other merchant, and not so quickly delivered."

I swept my eyes over the camp. There were hundreds of tents, but many had their flaps tightly shut with pins, long sewing needles, or even sticks. I nodded at them. "Why are they closed like that?"

Muffy followed where I looked and pursed her lips. "Those are the tents that belong to the sick people, but they haven't had much chance to use them. Their friends and neighbors helped set them up while they recover so they're near one another when they recover."

"How long does that take?"

She closed her eyes and shook her head. "I can't say. For the stronger ones like those of my age they're healthy in a few days, but the older people like many of the parents their recovery can take up to two weeks."

I glanced across the tents to the large sick house. "Is it safe to visit them?"

Muffy nodded. "Yes. It's only the air that makes them sick so they can't pass it on to anyone else."

"So it sounds like we'd be good candidates to lend a hand," I suggested.

Muffy tilted her head to one side and studied me. "Why do you wish to see the big tent?"

I grabbed her hand and gave her a wink. "Because a couple of young, pretty ladies coming in there are sure to bring some smiles to a few faces."

Darda rolled her eyes. "By all the gods. . ."

"No, by Miriam," I quipped. "And besides, with this many people out-" I swept my hand over the many shut tents, "-I think they could use all the hands that are offered." I glanced at Muffy. "What do you say?"

"It's a wonderful idea and they're always in need of extra hands, but-" she bit her lower lip and bowed her head.

I leaned to my right and caught her downcast gaze. "Is something wrong?"

"Could I. . .that is, I would dearly love to know your names," she pleaded.

I feigned a gasp. "We haven't introduced ourselves, have we?" I slipped in front of her and flourished my hand across my chest as I gave her a deep bow. "I'm Miriam, Maiden to Xander the Great and this-" I lifted my head and gestured to Darda, "-is my ever-present shadow companion, Darda."

Muffy smiled and bowed to me. "It's a pleasure to meet you, Miriam and Darda."

Darda frowned down at my poor-posture position. "As an ambassador you must take your role more seriously."

"I'm taking this-" I straightened and a twinge ran through my back that made me wince and put my voice into a higher octave, "-seriously."

"The gods are scolding you," she warned me.

"They can scold me all they want so long as they stay on their side of the pond," I quipped. I glanced at Muffy and smiled. "I'm ready for that big tent tour."

"But are you sure you wish to see it?" Muffy asked me.

I grabbed one of Darda's hands and one of hers, and tugged the pair toward the big tent, "If Miriam says she wants to go, then we green-light-go!"

I pulled my friends through the game board-style tent city and we soon found ourselves at one of the short ends of the large tent. Some twenty feet outside the sickness tent we found a familiar face. It was the young man Sala. He leaned against his spear and watched a group of children playing ball near the edge of the woods. A soft smile lay on his face as his eyes followed their laughing tussle over an inflated sheep's bladder.

He straightened at our coming and tipped his head to us. "A good afternoon to you, my ladies."

Our small group stopped before him. A light blush brightened Muffy's cheeks before she slipped behind me. I leaned to one side and looked past him at the interior of the tent. "Is Durion already inside?"

He nodded. "Yep. You can find him talking to the head nurse about the people. For myself-" he returned his attention to the children and a playful smile slipped across his lips, "-I'd rather be out there as young as those saplings."

Darda frowned at him. "Durion takes his responsibilities toward others very seriously. Too seriously to idle his time watching children."

He chuckled. "If that's what you have to worry about, then I guess yeah."

I gave him a lazy salute and took Muffy's hand with mine. "Well, thanks for the info."

We walked past him with Darda as our rear guard. As she brushed past the sentry I felt her stumble against my back. I stopped a few yards into the long tent and looked over my shoulder at her. Her intense gaze lay on Sala's back. "I don't think he's your type, Darda," I teased her.

She pursed her lips and shook her head. Her voice was so low even I could hardly hear it. "That young man looked at me with an unwarranted amount of disgust."

I shrugged. "Maybe he doesn't like dragons. I mean, some dragons don't like-" I took a step forward and nearly stumbled into Muffy who'd stopped in front of us and had half-turned.

"I'm so sorry!" she apologized as we caught each other by the shoulders.

"It's all right, but what were you-" I followed her line of sight and saw that her attention lay on the young Sala. My mischievous eyes flickered back to Muffy. Her blush brightened and she half-turned away from me. I nudged her a little in the arm. "He's kind of cute, isn't he?" She bowed her head, but nodded. "I think Mies said something about him coming recently?"

"Y-yes. Another hundred of our-that is, my people came from the desert two days ago," she told me.

I winked at her. "*Our* people is just fine. After all, we humans have to stick close in this world."

She studied me and furrowed her brow. "But aren't Maidens dragons?"

"They *can* be if they go through a ceremony," I told her.

"And you haven't done that?"

I shook my head. "Not yet. We're-well, we're still working on things outside the castle."

The air inside the large tent was stifling. Cots lined either side of a narrow hall, and most of them were occupied by patients who exhibited severe signs of an allergy epidemic. Their eyes were bloodshot, and they sniffled and sneezed until I wondered how they kept their noses on. Several women hurried from bed-to-bed handing out handkerchiefs and taking the well-used ones to a large, short tub filled with the tidings of ill health. They all wore aprons and long looks to denote their role as caretakers of the sick and recovering.

We found Durion at the bedside of a man of forty. His red runny nose denoted him as one of the ill, though unlike the others he wore a clean set of clothes with a small pendant around his neck. A nurse stood nearby, and from her stiff posture and tired eyes I guessed she was one of the leads in this battle against illness.

"And you're sure this will work?" the man asked Durion.

Durion smiled and nodded. "Absolutely. We give nothing else to our visitors who fall ill, and within a few days they are themselves."

The man looked down at himself and smiled. "Well, I suppose as head of the tent and a resident of one of the beds I had best try the mix on myself first."

"Is that wise, doctor?" the nurse wondered as her eyes flickered over to Durion. "Perhaps one of the other patients should be the first."

The doctor laughed, but his amusement was interrupted by a violent sneezing fit. He wiped a trail of snot from his upper lip before he shook his head. "No. If this is a sure-fired quick cure I'd like to be the first to try it myself, if only to do away with these-" he commented as he lifted his limp, well-used handkerchief.

She pursed her lips, but nodded. "Then I will find the ingredients myself."

"My people would be better positioned to find them," Durion pointed out.

She scowled at him. "Do you think I'm not capable of recognizing these herbs?"

He shook his head. "Not at all, but the forest is a dangerous place and I have a few men out there who would gladly fetch the ingredients in quick time."

The doctor grasped one of his hands in his own and smiled up at Durion. "Thank you for the offer, and we gratefully accept." His eyes flickered to the disgruntled woman. "Don't we?" She stiffened, spun on her heels, and marched off. He sighed and dropped his hands into his lap. "She'll be grateful when your medicine works."

"What medicine?" I inquired as we walked up to the pair.

Durion turned to us and smiled before he bowed his head. "Neito Vedesta, and Lady Darda, what a pleasure to see you both." At his speaking my Maiden of the Water title

Muffy looked up at me and furrowed her brow. "What has brought you here?"

"We were wondering if we could help," I told him.

The doctor chuckled. "You might be too late. Your friend here told us about this elixir that's supposed to cure the-" he furrowed his brow and looked up at Durion, "-what was the name?"

"Metsä Nenä," he replied.

The doctor wrinkled his nose. "What a strange name."

"It means 'Forest Nose,'" Muffy spoke up. We all looked at her, and she shrank beneath our gazes. "At least, I think it does. . ."

Durion smiled at her before he nodded. "You are correct, but I am surprised a young girl such as yourself knows the ancient fae tongue."

"I-I read a lot," she admitted.

"Your studies have proven successful," he complimented her before he returned his attention to the doctor. "I will inform my men of the needed supplies and will return shortly with them."

The doctor bowed his head. "Thank-*achoo*!" He wiped the trail of snot from his upper lip and sighed. "Thank you."

Durion bowed his head. "The pleasure is all mine. If you will excuse me." He turned to us, made a quick head-bow, and hurried in the direction that we came.

The doctor turned his full attention to us and smiled. "So you'd like to help. We could always use such pretty little ladies in here." I nudged Darda in the arm and grinned at her. She rolled her eyes, but said nothing. He nodded at the head nurse who sulked in the far end of the sick tent. "You can speak with her and see if she needs-" his face wrinkled up before a powerful sneeze erupted from his nose. He covered his nose with his handkerchief and waved his hand at the nurse. "Her."

FOREST OF THE DRAGON

We nodded and walked down the long rows of beds to the opposite end of the tent. A few long, short tables stood against the canvas wall, and stacked high on their tops were handkerchiefs and bedding. Some of the handkerchiefs were newly washed and lay in a woven basket. The woman, like a machine, plucked one out, folded it with a few quick motions, and set the handkerchief on a rising stack of ready ones.

I sidled up to her with my friends behind me, but she didn't look up. I cleared my throat. "Um, hi."

She paused in her work and glared up at me. "What do you want?"

"We were wondering if we could help out here," I explained.

Her eyes narrowed as she studied Darda and me. "I don't know you. Are you new arrivals?"

I sheepishly grinned at her as I shook my head. "Well, not exactly. We came in with the fae ambassadors and-"

The woman leapt to her feet and literally stood toe-to-toe with me. "I don't need any more of your 'help,' now leave."

I frowned. "But-"

She stabbed a finger at the exit. "Get out, or I'll be forced to throw you out!"

I held up my hands. "All right, we're leaving, we're leaving. Sheesh. . ." I muttered as we passed by her and out of the tent.

And so ended my philanthropic attempt. Not with a whimper, but with a shout. A shrill one.

CHAPTER 8

Darda took the snub tougher than I did as she balled her hands into fists at her sides and stomped past me. "The insolence! She is nothing more than a-a-" she stood to her full short stature and quivered, "-an unforgivable, stupid vampiri de hârtie!"

I stopped in my tracks and blinked at her. "A what?"

Muffy stepped up to my side and joined me in watching Darda stomp to and fro in front of us. "Those are a species of bats that are native to the northwestern islands. They're often fired from cannons and can drain their victim dry in a minute."

I winced. "Right. Those things."

She whipped her head up to me and her eyes widened. "You've seen them?"

I snorted. "Seen them? I watched Tillit fire off those things at a bunch of Red Dragons."

FOREST OF THE DRAGON

She stepped closer to me and clasped her hands against her chest as I'd seen her do before. "Please tell me, do they really look like paper?"

I nodded. "Yeah, and their paper cuts are the worst in the world." I paused and frowned. "At least I hope so."

"What else have you seen? The mathair shuigh of the Golden realm? Or maybe some Hallita Fly from the island of Villi Saaret?"

I dropped my hands onto her shoulders and smiled down at her. "I've seen a lot of things, but one thing I haven't seen yet is a human wind user."

She blinked up at me. "A human user? Then have you seen a rare dragon magic user?"

I sheepishly grinned at her. "Well, let's just say I've seen it used, but I want you to show me how *you* use it."

She shrank beneath my hold and bit her lower lip. "I'm. . .I'm not that good at it. . ."

"But the priests did teach you?" I asked her.

She averted her eyes from mine and nodded. "Yes, but-well, I sometimes can't control it."

"That's not a problem," I assured her as I swept my eyes over the area. I found my target and snatched Muffy's hand. "Come on." We dove into the thicket of tents, leaving my old friend behind.

"Miriam!" Darda shouted as she hurried to catch up. "Where are you going? We cannot leave without Xander."

"We're not leaving, we're just going some place with fewer casualties," I told her.

Her mouth dropped open. "Fewer what?"

"*Tent* casualties," I corrected myself as I stopped us at the edge of the clearing. The nearest tents were some hundred feet off and no human was nearer than them. I released Muffy and turned to face her with a smile. "Is this enough room?"

She bit her lower lip as she studied the area. "I-I think so. I mean, I can't make that much wind. . ."

Darda looked between us with a frown. "What is going on here?"

I stepped back away from Muffy to stand beside Darda and gestured to our new friend. "Muffy here is going to show us some wind magic."

Muffy shrank beneath our gazes. "I-I don't know-"

"What can it hurt to try?" I asked her.

Darda glanced over our shoulders at the canvas tents staked to the ground and pursed her lips. "A great deal."

I nudged her in the arm and glared at her. "Give Muffy a little credit."

"Credit must be earned," she countered.

I returned my attention to Muffy and smiled at her. "You heard Darda, Muff. Time to earn some credit."

Muffy bit her lower lip, but gave a nod. She stretched out her arms in front of her and cupped her hands together before she scrunched her eyes shut. A shimmer of air movement appeared in her cupped hands. That shimmer transformed into a mini tornado hardly larger than a soup bowl. The eye of the storm was so small that I couldn't have slipped my arm inside.

Muffy peeked open one eye. Her face lit up as she glimpsed the tiny bundle of destruction in her hands. "I did it!" She whipped her head up to her smiling friends. "I did it! I made a wind devil!"

Darda bowed her head. "And a very beautiful one, Miss Mufid."

I pointed at her triumph. "So how big can those wind devils get?"

Muffy winced. "Well, to be honest I was trying to make this one ten feet tall, but-well, I'm not very good at conjuring them."

I shrugged. "It's not a bad little wind devil, and you didn't lose control."

A gentle breeze blew past us and swept over Muffy's hands. The naturally moving air swiped the small tornado from her grasp and flew away into the trees with the mini tornado in its clutches. The kidnapper and kidnapped disappeared into the forest, leaving Muffy crestfallen.

She looked at where it had gone before she turned back to us with a sad shake of her head. "That almost always happens. A wind takes my wind and Father Darbat scolds me and makes me do it again, but I still don't get any better."

I furrowed my brow. "You know, when I use my- ow!" Darda had sent a well-aimed, bony elbow into my ribs. "What was that for?"

"Prudence, Miriam," she reminded me.

I rolled my eyes before I looked back to Muffy. "Anyway, how about you try again, but with more feeling?"

She tilted her head at me and blinked her eyes. "Feeling? Father Darbat says I need to focus my mind on the wind."

"Well, how about trying to *feel* the wind. You know, how it feels across your cheeks and stuff. How it might make you smile on a hot day," I suggested.

Muffy furrowed her brow, but gave a nod. "I'll try." She held out her hands as before and closed her eyes.

A soft tremor made me look down at my feet with a furrowed brow. "Um, can your winds move the ground?"

Muffy opened her eyes and shook her head. "I'm not strong enough for that unless its desert sands. Why do you ask?"

I pointed at the ground. "Because I just felt-"

A jagged crack some five feet long developed in the ground where my finger pointed. Muffy and I stepped back as the earth began to shake beneath us. Darda grabbed the backs of our collars and yanked us backward hard enough that she threw us into herself. We toppled to the ground and watched as the crack split open into a ten foot round hole.

From the hole emerged a grassy horror. It had stump legs-literally legs made of stumps-that were attached to a turtle-like body that was made of a thick grass and covered in multiples layers of bark that made a shell. Its head was a gray boulder with a pair of jaws and large eyes hewn from orange crystals.

The thing climbed out of the hole one stumpy step at a time until it faced us. We gave it ample space, but the creature stretched out its neck like a giraffe and opened its jaws wide. The space between the jaws could have fit me and had enough room for a couple of anvils. I didn't want either dropping on my head, so I took a step back and raised my hand to sweep the creature away with a blast of water.

Darda grabbed my wrist and pushed my arm down as she looked into my eyes. "You mustn't!"

I glared back at her. "If I don't then we'll all be killed!"

Darda looked up into the sky and smiled. "There is no need."

A shadow flew over us and forced my attention to the sky. Xander in all his winged glory unsheathed his sword Bucephalus and dropped down atop the beast. He embedded his weapon deep into the top of the woody skull of the creature. The thing lifted his head and let loose a terrible screeching roar that shook the leaves on the trees.

The ground shook and more cracks appeared in the empty area. A half dozen more stumpy creatures emerged and stalked over to us.

The beast Xander had subdued swung its head to and fro to dislodge him. He drew out Bucephalus and leapt down in front of us so he faced the beast and its new comrades. Grass grew over the wound atop its head, wiping away his effort in a few seconds.

"What in all the realms is that thing?" a voice yelped behind us.

I looked over my shoulder and saw that a great many of the humans had gathered at the edge of the tents. At the front stood Mies, and beside him was his daughter and Durion. Around them was a small contingent of guards who held up their spears with the knowledge that they were toothpicks compared to the tree creatures that stood before them. Along the front lines of humans was Father Darbat who gaped at the creature with wide eyes.

Tillit was nearly as flabbergasted, but he managed a whistle. "That is a very ugly tree."

Durion's mouth was agape as he beheld the behemoths. "That's impossible! The taimet vanished after the war and could not be summoned again!"

Mies whipped his head to Durion and glared at him. "Even I know the word 'sapling' when I hear it! So this is your doing!"

"Send your people to the keep!" Xander ordered Mies as his eyes fell on Durion. "How can we defeat these beasts?"

Durion shook his head. "I do not know. They were not defeated in the war by the humans, and we ourselves never had to subdue them."

The lead creature roared and stomped toward we three girls. Its brethren followed suit so that the earth trembled beneath their march.

"Lord Mies, your people!" Xander shouted.

Mies pursed his lips, but whipped his head to one of the guards. "Get these people to the keep! Now!" The soldier saluted and, with his fellow men, began the process of herding the citizens to safety.

Meanwhile, Darda, Muffy and I were definitely *not* in safety as the taimet quickened their pace so that they became a stampede. We turned tail and ran.

Tillit raised his arms above his head and his voice boomed over the distance between us. "Over here, you sons of rotten bark! Come and get me, you bunch of overgrown weeds!"

Durion cupped his hands over his mouth and joined the chorus. "To me, beasts of grass!"

Tillit looked at him with a frown. "Is that all you have?"

Durion pursed his lips, cupped his hands against and took a deep breath. "Come to me, you children of hoary stock!"

Tillit grinned. "That's better."

No amount of shouting, waving, or insults would distract the creatures from us. The behemoths were faster than they looked, too, and cut off our escape through the trees. Muffy lagged behind, so Xander swooped down and slipped his arms beneath her. He had her lifted her some ten feet off the ground before one of the creatures tilted its head back and opened its jaws.

"Xander!" Durion shouted. "Behind you!"

Xander glanced over his shoulder in time to watch the beast loose a green loogie at him. They were round balls comprised of grass and rocks. He dodged the first one and flew another fifty feet higher, but the beast fired like a rapid machine gun. One of the balls him him in the back and shoved him forward. He lost his grip on Muffy and she fell screaming to the air.

I whipped my head to Darda as we continued our arch around the perimeter of the clearing. "Now?"

She nodded. "Now!"

I flung up one of my arms and the water wrapped around my body slipped up my arm and launched into the air as a thick column. Muffy landed rear-first on the top and I cut my arm in front of me. The column followed and deposited her on the ground on her feet, but her legs shook so much that she collapsed.

Darda and I reached her, and she looked up at me with wide eyes. "Neito Vedesta," she whispered.

"I think enough people know that," I quipped as I spun around to face our pursuers.

FOREST OF THE DRAGON

I raised both arms and serpentine dragons slipped up them to tower over me. They loosed their roars before they plunged downward in an arch at the beasts. Dragon met plant, and dragon wasn't the winner. The plant creatures absorbed the water, and I even felt a tug as more of my clothing was drawn from me through the connection.

I broke the connection and looked at Darda. "Running time again!"

CHAPTER 9

Muffy still sat on the ground. Darda and I slipped one of our arms beneath hers and yanked her to her feet.

The beasts continued to follow us as Darda nodded at the tents with their wide pathways. "We may be able to hide in there."

"Good," I wheezed as I tried to catch my breath.

We raced into the tents and reached the first intersection. Only one of the taimet followed us into the mess. The others stopped on the edge and snorted. One of them tilted back its head and launched another loogie, but this one was without the rocks. The muck arched toward us. Darda shoved Muffy and me out of the way, and was a direct casualty as the much slammed into the intersection.

"Darda!" I screamed.

The dust settled and revealed Darda's head in the ball, but everything else was buried. She wiggled and grimaced. "Save yourself! I cannot move!"

FOREST OF THE DRAGON

I rushed forward, but another loogie-this one with rocks-blocked my path to her. Three of the other four taimet that stood at the edge hocked their own loogies and dropped them on the other points around Darda, creating a crude 'x.'

I furrowed my brow, but a noise made me spin around. The taimi that had followed us took a position in the intersection behind us and dug into the ground so that only its shell was visible.

My mouth dropped open. "Is this-"

"Terni lapilli!" Tillit shouted at me.

I blinked at him. "What?"

"Three stones at a time! It's a-"

My eyes widened. "Game! It's tic-tac-toe!"

One of the other taimet moved from its place off the board and started a quick march up the rows to the intersection above us. I grabbed Muffy's hand. "Follow me and just do what I tell you!"

"What?" she yelped as I dragged her up the rows as the taimi matched us speed-for-speed. We reached the intersection first because it had to turn.

"Stay here!" I ordered her.

She whipped her head to the taimi and cringed. "But-"

"Stay!"

I raced to the intersection one higher than Muffy, and two higher than Darda. That would give us three in a row, and a win. Muffy crouched down and covered her head with her hands as the taimi that had lost its intersection to her rushed her position. Our opponent swept past her and raced up the same path as me, but at a faster speed. I threw balls of water at its face, but they might as well have been splashes of rain.

The taimi passed over me and was nearly at the intersection. I threw a trail of water in front of me and leapt into a hitter's slide. With the aid of my moving water I reached the intersection at the same time as the taimi. It lowered itself to burrow into the ground, but I threw up a couple of columns of water on one side of its body and tilted it off its stubby legs and onto its back.

The creature gave a mournful cry as I stood up, placed my hands on my hip, and grinned at my defeated foe. "We win."

The taimet all gave sorrowful cries before they burrowed into the earth, leaving nothing but soft dirt behind them. The beast I had tipped onto its back tried to right itself, but remained stuck.

I took a step toward it when the earth shook. A crack opened beneath the taimi and swallowed the creature whole. Another shake and the crack slammed shut, leaving only a risen scar of dirt and grass.

I leaned against one of the nearby tents and wiped my brow as Xander dropped from the sky. He grasped my shoulders and looked me over. "Are you unhurt?"

I nodded. "Everything but my pride. Those damn things didn't even blink when I shot my water into their eyes."

"That is because they do not truly have eyes," Durion spoke up as Tillit and he joined us. "They are the forest made flesh, or at least as flesh as one could make rock, grass, and tree."

Xander glanced over at him. "Do you have any idea what could have caused the taimet to rise at this moment-"

"-and play a game with us," I added.

He shook his head. "I cannot fathom how this might have happened."

Tillit's eyes flickered to Xander and he twitched his nose. "You don't happen to be around here looking for something other than peace, do you?"

Durion arched an eyebrow and glanced between Tillit and Xander as my dragon lord pursed his lips. "Is there some ulterior motive of which I am unaware?"

"Miriam!" Darda shouted as she, with Muffy behind her, rushed up to me. She was still covered in a thick layer of the gunk, but she still grasped my hands and looked me over. "Are you unhurt?"

I snorted. "I'm fine, but you look like something sneezed on you."

She looked down at herself and wrinkled her nose. "I might still be trapped in that foul-smelling ball if you had not realized what was occurring."

I jerked my head toward Tillit. "He sealed the deal for me."

Tillit puffed out his chest. "It pays to be among children."

"And to have the mind of a child," Darda quipped.

"I would appreciate if you would all be forthcoming in your reasons for coming with me to Virea Metsa," Durion pleaded.

Xander opened his mouth, but a noise at the other end of the tent caught our attention. Mies stomped through the tent city with Sala on one side, Valo on the other, and Father Darbat at his back. Behind their group were two dozen guards. He stopped before us and glared at Durion. "Is this how you repay our hospitality?"

Durion frowned. "You cannot believe that I nor my people were involved in this attack."

"Those were your weapons in the Great Exile!" Mies snapped as he jabbed a finger at the father. "Darbat confirmed it!"

"They were used against you in the war, yes, but my people have been unable to use such magic for thousands of years!" Durion insisted.

"How do you intend to prove me wrong?" Mies snapped.

Durion's eyes flickered to Valo. She clasped her hands together in front of her as though in supplication. He took a deep breath and returned his attention to Mies. "In a sign of trust I will allow myself to not only remain here, but for some of your own people to go in my place to Metsan Keskella to present your terms to the king."

"Durion!" Xander scolded him.

Durion turned to Xander and shook his head. "I can think of no other way, old friend. Though my father will be angry, you must explain to him that for the good of both people I made this small sacrifice of my freedom."

Mies scoffed. "What is a lowly guard leader to me? And how can I be sure my own people won't be held captive in your city?"

Xander stepped forward. "I will guarantee their safety."

The human lord's face softened at Xander, but he still pursed his lips as he looked back to Durion. "That still doesn't tell me why you'd be so valuable to me."

Durion stretched himself to his full height. "Because I am Prince Durion of the Arbor Fae, only son of King Thorontur."

Mies's eyes widened and there came an audible gasp from Valo. A sly smile slipped onto the human lord's lips as he folded his arms across his wide chest. "I see now. The king is stupid enough to have his own child come into the enemy camp."

"Father!" Valo scolded him before she gestured to Durion. "He was very kind to come himself to speak with us, and have you forgotten that he saved many of our people from those beasts?"

"That could've been a ruse to fool us," he argued.

Valo's eyes fell on Durion and a smile slipped onto her lips as she shook her head. "No. An honest face such as his can't lie."

Mies's shoulders drooped and his face fell. "Truly?" She turned to him and nodded. He pulled at his beard for a moment before he shook his head. "Well, you have the intuition of your mother, gods bless her, so I'll take your word for it."

Valo bowed her head to him. "Thank you, Father."

"Then do you accept my offers?" Durion asked him.

Mies nodded. "I accept." His eyes flickered to his smiling daughter and he sighed. "I have to." He cleared his throat and stood straight and tall. "Now then, as my ambassadors I choose-"

"Me," Valo spoke up.

Mies frowned at her. "That's going too far, my little naqia."

"Our friends the fae offered up as their ambassador their own prince. It's only fitting we should do the same," she pointed out before she gestured to Xander. "And Lord Xander has already offered to protect anyone who comes with him." Xander bowed his head. Her eyes settled on me. "Besides, a female ambassador won't be looked upon as hostile."

Mies pursed his lips. "I know I can't stop you when you put your mind to it, but if I can't convince you to stay-" she smiled and shook her head, "-then I'll decide who joins you." He swept his eyes over the crowd and gestured to Sala. "Sala will go with you. His sharp eyes won't miss any of the wily tricks of the fae, and Father Darbat-" he turned to the priest, "-who would you choose to represent your group within we humans?"

The father furrowed his brow. "I don't believe I'll choose anyone to-"

"I will go," Muffy spoke up.

Darbat's eyes widened as they fell on the meek girl. "You?" he scoffed. "You hardly know wind magic."

"Then the fae won't see her as a threat," I spoke up before I moved to stand by her side. I draped an arm over her shoulders and smiled down at her. "We can have a human's night out on the old fae town."

Father Darbat studied me with a hard expression. "I'd hardly call you a human, not with those powerful water skills you used fighting those-those things. In my experience that looked more like fae magic."

Mies eyes me with a critical eye before his eyes flickered to Xander. "Were you trying to trick me into thinking she was a human so I'd believe you more, or did you really think I wouldn't notice?"

Xander stood to his full height and stared at Mies with an unblinking gaze. "I have Miriam by my side because she is my Maiden, and whether or not she is fae or human does not matter to me."

"But it matters to me," Mies argued. His daughter opened her mouth to speak, but he held up his hand toward her. "Not on this point, Valo. This is treachery."

"I think Lord Xander prefers the term 'omission,'" Tillit spoke up.

Mies glared at him. "Would you go against me, too?"

Tillit held up his hands in front of him and shook his head. "I'm not going against anybody, but if you think Miriam here is some kind of threat to you then you might want to remember that it was Xander and she who stopped that coup at Hadia."

Mies stiffened his lower jaw, but turned his attention to Sala. "Get ready to leave with Lady Valo, and whatever you do don't leave her side outside of this camp, got it?"

Sala smiled and bowed his head. "Perfectly."

Mies glanced at our group and narrowed his eyes as his gaze set on Xander. "Her life is also in your hands, dragon. Don't disappoint me, or more than the fae will have to answer for the consequences."

Xander bowed his head. "I understand."

"I hope so." Mies turned and stomped away with his entourage. Only Valo remained.

Durion walked up to the young woman and bowed his head to her. "Thank you, Lady Valo, for your kindness."

She smiled and shook her head. "I was merely following your example, Your Highness."

His eyes flickered up to her. "I would much rather you call me Durion, Lady Valo."

She laughed. "Then you must call me Valo."

I sidled up to Xander who stood off from the lovebirds watching them. I leaned close to him and lowered my voice to a whisper. "I think there's more than just sickness in this forest air."

He looked down at me and smiled. "This ancient forest holds many secret talents." His smile faltered as he glanced over his shoulder at Darda. Muffy was vainly trying to help her pull the ooze from her person. "I fear the greatest secret is far from finished with us."

I frowned up at him. "Don't ruin the mood." I glanced at the couple and the loving way they look at each other. "If they're not careful the whole world is going to know their secret and-" my eyes flickered over to the direction where Mies had gone, "-I don't think the prospective fathers-in-law will like it."

"Many wars have been averted and alliances made through matrimony," he pointed out before he looked over at the thick canopy of trees and pursed his lips. "Unfortunately, another source may not grant them enough time to even exchange their vows."

CHAPTER 10

Tillit walked up to us and hitched up his pants as he gave us a curious look. "So what's it this time? Vampires running amok? Werewolves butting in on each other's territories? Giant squid trying to make inroads into the mainland?"

I blinked at him. "Is that possible?"

He wrinkled his nose. "I hope not, but I've seen those giant squid do some strange things."

"We are here to assist in the peace between fae and humans," Xander told him.

Tillit snorted. "And Cayden is naming his baby after me, and speaking of which they granted me the honor of telling you that Stephanie had her child. A healthy baby girl." He paused and rubbed his chin in one hand. "Come to think of it, it's probably a good thing they didn't name it after me. Two beautiful creatures in the world with the name of Tillit would be too much."

FOREST OF THE DRAGON

Durion and Valo walked up to our group, and our fae friend's gaze settled on Xander. "You have not answered my question, old friend, regarding all the reasons you came to the forest."

A crooked smile slipped onto Xander's lips. "Would you believe that we may be chasing a god?"

Durion arched an eyebrow. "If you had asked me that same question only a half hour before I would have answered 'no,' but after witnessing the rise of the taimet I would be ready to believe that divine intervention may be at play. But-" his eyes flickered between Xander and me, "-have you both achieved such strength that you are no capable of defeating a god?"

Xander shook his head. "We cannot defeat them, merely return them to their own world." He turned his attention to Valo. "My Lady, might I inquire if anything unusual has happened to your people since you came to the forest?"

She shook her head. "Nothing at all save for what you yourselves have seen. But tell me, Lord Xander, what is this god capable of? Should I tell my father-"

"Tell him nothing until we are sure ," Xander warned her before he swept his eyes over the tent area. The humans were only now trailing back into their homes. "I would not frighten your people without just cause."

"Then can you tell *me* what we're up against?" she pleaded.

"If this is another god then it's different from the last one we were up against," I spoke up. "Well, two gods. They were wind users, but whoever called those overgrown stumps up must be able to use magic like the fae around here."

Durion clenched one hand at his side and frowned. "If I could but use the powers of old then I know I would be of greater use to you."

Xander set a hand on his shoulder. "At the moment your people need you more, though I wish you had chosen a different method to help them. Your father will not be pleased."

"But my father was very pleased," Valo assured him as her soft eyes flickered up to Durion's face. "He would not have accepted any less a noble figure to remain, and now I have the chance to confer with their noble king."

Xander looked to her with a smile and bowed his head. "I accept the beautiful correction, My Lady."

I frowned and jabbed him in the ribs with my elbow. "Are we forgetting that your Maiden was almost flattened by an overgrown paper weight?"

"Um, My Lady?" Muffy's meek voice spoke up. I turned to her and found her looking up at me with curious eyes. "Are you really a fae?"

I shrugged. "Only half."

Tillit snorted. "There are some full fae who don't have as much power as you do." He noticed Durion's downcast expression and pursed his lips. "Not that there's anything wrong with that. Besides, Miriam didn't exactly get all that water power the easy way. She-"

"Quiet!" Darda hissed.

Tillit wrinkled his piggish nose. "Now you're going to keep Tillit from telling the best story he has?"

Darda paid him no heed. Her eyes lay on a block of tents to our left as she drew out one dagger and crept close to the flap. She threw open the cloth door and revealed a crouching Sala.

He sheepishly grinned up at her as she put away her weapon. "Looks like you caught me."

"Sala, why are you in there?" Valo scolded him.

He stepped out and straightened. "Your father told me to watch you, but I thought sitting there would be more fun. Like a game of hide-and-find."

Durion frowned at the young man. "Protecting your Lady Valo is a matter not to be taken lightly."

Sala shrugged. "I think life is too serious to be taken seriously, but don't worry about Lady Valo. I won't let anything happen to her."

Valo smiled at him. "Thank you, Sala. Have the preparations been made?"

He nodded. "Mostly. Your father wants everyone, but especially him-" he nodded at Durion, "-to meet him at the front gates. The horses are waiting there."

"And my men?" Durion asked him.

"They're there, too."

Durion stood to his full height and looked in the direction of the gate of the keep. "Then I won't keep them waiting any longer."

The fae prince led our large group around the ruined walls of the keep to the front where the main gate had once stood. A temporary door of sliced planks stood half-finished in the mouth of the gate, and on either side were the ruins of the guard towers. Our horses, taken from us on our capture, waited for us along with three others for Sala, Valo, and Muffy.

Also among the steeds were two fae soldiers, the observers who Sala had so expertly found. At seeing them Durion hurried forward and grasped their hands. "I am glad to see you."

One of them nodded. "As are we, captain, but they have told us you are not to return with us to the city."

Durion shook his head. "No, at least not yet. You need not worry for me. I am sure I will be home in a very short time. There is a favor I wish to ask of you."

"Anything."

"Tell my father that my wish is for him to listen to this young woman-" he half-turned to Valo and gestured to her, "-and see if her words do not show the kindness of which the humans are capable. Those are my words I wish for you to pass on to my father." The men nodded.

Mies was among the men preparing the pair of horses with a few provisions, but at our coming he strode over to us and glanced at Durion. "Are you ready to accept our agreement?"

Durion nodded. "I am."

"Good." He nodded at a pair of guards. They surrounded Durion on both sides.

"Must he have guards?" Valo asked her father.

"Not for long. If he treats them right we'll treat him right," he assured her. He nodded at the guards, and they bowed their heads in return before they marched Durion off.

The love-struck fae looked over his shoulder at us, and most especially Valo, before the three turned a corner and disappeared out of sight.

Xander set his hand on Valo and she looked up at him with pursed lips. He smiled down at her. "Let us go now to Metsan Keskella." She swallowed and gave a nod to him.

Tillit had parted from our company, but soon returned with one of his strange cat-donkeys. He noticed my staring and smiled at me as he patted the creature on the nose. "You won't find a gentler eselkatze in all the realms. I raised her myself from an eselkatzchen and brought her out for this special trip."

I blinked at him. "A what?"

He chuckled. "A young eselkatze is called an eselkatzchen. In the tongue of the hairy dragons that means 'kitten.'"

I blinked at him. "'Hairy dragons?'"

"My name for the dragons under the brown banner," he explained. He wrinkled his piggish snout. "Everything about them is brown, even their stench."

We mounted our steeds and turned them toward the fae city. Mies followed us for a few yards waving at his little girl. A few tears glistened in his eyes. Behind him came

FOREST OF THE DRAGON

Father Darbat who watched with apprehension as his novice apprentice left with us.

We traveled through the woods and within a few hours found ourselves before the grand fae city of Metsan Keskella. The reception at the gate was foreboding, mostly because I'd never seen so many armed guards mounted on horses and lined up in long columns behind them.

At the head of the army, atop a snow-white horse, was the fae king himself, Thorontur. At our coming he and a small entourage rode up and met us some twenty yards from the gates.

"Durion's horse returned some time ago, but I do not see my son among your party. Where is he?" he questioned Xander.

Xander's eyes flickered to the tense rows and columns of fae soldiers. "This would be better spoken of in private."

Thorontur glared at him. "I will have it out now, or you will never enter my city again."

"He is a guest of Lord Mies, leader of the humans," Xander told him.

The father's face paled and his hands that tightly held the reins turned white. "A hostage?"

"A willing trade," Xander countered.

"A trade? For what?" Thorontur snapped.

"For me, King Thorontur," Valo spoke up.

He whipped his head to her and narrowed his eyes. "What worth could you have, human?"

"I am Valo Mies, daughter to Lord Mies, and I have come in your son's place to plead peace," she revealed.

"Peace!" Thorontur shouted so loud that his horse threw its head back and neighed. "What peace can be had while my son is a prisoner of the enemy?"

Valo sat calmly in the face of the fae king's anger. "Your son is a very noble man, King Thorontur, and he wished for me to explain our position-"

"You have no position! Your are trespassing in this forest!" Thorontur snapped.

Xander narrowed his eyes at the fae king. "Do I not also have a say in who may reside in this forest?"

Thorontur whipped his head to him and his eyebrows crashed down. "Does my own emissary turn against me?"

Xander shook his head. "No. I would only remind you that to start a needless war is an outcome even your own people would sacrifice much to avoid."

"They will heed this cause as they have in the past!" Thorontur argued.

I swept my eyes over the pale faces of the fae soldiers as they shifted from foot-to-foot. "I don't think they're thinking that right now." Thorontur clenched his teeth so hard that I swear I heard them crack.

Valo maneuvered her horse around us and over to Thorontur. His guards surrounded him and drew out their swords, but she didn't stop until the nose of her horse brushed against the noses of theirs. She met Thorontur's harsh gaze with her soft one, and smiled at him.

"You have your son's kind eyes, King Thorontur." The fae ruler's tense face relaxed a little under such kind words. "I have known your son for but a short time, but I know he would wish for you to keep his men from war."

Thorontur shook his head. "I do not believe a word that you speak, human."

"What about your son's words?" I spoke up.

Thorontur looked to me and frowned. "What do you mean? Is he here?"

I nodded at the two fae guards who were a part of our group. "He told them to give you a message."

The king whipped his head to the pair. "Well! Out with it!"

One of them cleared his throat. "Prince Durion instructed us to tell you, in his own words, that 'my wish is for him to listen to this young woman-" he nodded at Valo as

Durion had done, "-and see if her words do not show the kindness of which the humans are capable.'"

Thorontur's face fell. He leaned back on his steed and pursed his lips. His guards behind him waited in tense anticipation. Our group held our breath.

Well, except for me. I rolled my eyes. "Come on. What could it hurt to listen to her? I mean, if you got these guys-" I swept my arm over the army, "-out this fast than you can get them out again when she's done talking."

Thorontur frowned at me, but turned his steed toward the city. "I will listen to her, but I promise nothing else."

CHAPTER 11

The columns parted and Thorontur led us up the winding green streets to his castle in the tree. Our steeds were taken to the stables and we to the throne room. Well, almost to the throne room.

At the tall doors to the throne room Thorontur stopped and half-turned to Xander. "Your Maiden may remain outside until we are through with this diplomatic charade."

Xander frowned. "Miriam is-"

"Not welcome in my throne room. At least for the time being," Thorontur persisted.

I shrugged. "That's fine. I need to go show Muffy the sights, anyway."

Thorontur arched an eyebrow. "Who is 'Muffy?'"

I slipped behind Muffy and grasped her shoulders before I peeked around her with a grin. "*This* is a Muffy. A one-of-a-kind human woman. One who doesn't like to talk."

FOREST OF THE DRAGON

Thorontur couldn't stop a small snort that escaped his lips. "That is indeed a rarity. I. . .I wish you both well in seeing our wonderful city." His attention next turned to Valo and her guard, Sala. He nodded at the young man. "I would also prefer you not bring your guard inside. The throne room is a sacred place where no blood has ever been shed, and to allow an outside guard would be an insult to me and my people."

Valo looked at Sala. "Would you mind waiting outside?"

He shrugged. "Sure." He sauntered over to a nearby wall and leaned his back against it.

The guards of the doors opened them, and Thorontur nodded at those who filed behind him. "Now let us hear what this human has to say." He turned and proceeded into his throne room.

Xander grasped my hands and pursed his lips as he watched the king lead the parade into the grand hall. "I am sorry for his behavior. He is not himself."

I shrugged. "It's fine. I'm not very good at this diplomatic stuff, anyway. You go in and try to prevent a world war, okay?" He nodded, and reluctantly left me.

The others passed by me with one of them being Valo. I held up my thumb to her and smiled. She paused and tilted her head to one side to study my gesture. "What does that mean?"

"It means 'good luck, we're all counting on you,'" I told her.

She smiled and bowed her head to me. "Thank you."

Soon the whole party had passed through the doors, and they shut behind them. I leaned toward Darda who stood beside me and lowered my voice to a whisper. "Do you think she'll be able to find Thorontur's sanity?"

Darda frowned as her eyes flickered up to me. "He has not lost anything, Miriam. He is merely concerned about his people."

"So concerned that he's keeping one of his most important assets out of a meeting of vital importance?" I countered.

A flicker of a mischievous smile slipped onto her lips. "He no doubt wishes to save the others in attendance from the horrors of listening to you snore halfway through the meeting."

I snorted. "Okay, I deserved that one."

Darda bowed her head. "You did indeed."

A meek voice interrupted our teasing. "Excuse me?" We turned our heads to find our shy companion Muffy standing nearby. Her wide eyes tried to take in both us and all of our surroundings at the same time, and she ended up looking dizzy and cross-eyed at the same time. "How large is this city?"

"Like population size?" I asked her.

She nodded. "Yes, and how many buildings there are, and how old they are. Everything."

I shook my head. "I have no idea."

"Nor do I," Darda chimed in.

Muffy's face fell. "Oh. I thought perhaps there might be a library or sage I might talk to."

A thought struck me. I looked over her short head at Darda and grinned. "How about we take her to see *them*? They might have Muffy's answers."

Darda wrinkled her nose. "Who do you mean?"

I jerked my head in the direction of the trunk. "You know, those guys in the trunk."

Her face fell and she frowned at me. "Miriam, that is no way to speak of such respected elders."

I looped my arm through one of Muffy's and began our walk toward the trunk, leaving Darda behind. "It's fine if you don't want to come."

"I said no such thing!" Darda huffed as she hurried after us.

FOREST OF THE DRAGON

Though it had been many months since my single last visit, I still remembered that the trunk of the tree had a hollow ring twenty feet wide and as tall. In the inner core were many doors, four total in the cardinal directions again, and more guards.

I led my small cabal around the circular hollow to the western door, and we stepped inside. The room we entered was the size of a small auditorium, but the ceiling was only ten feet high. From the ceiling hung pots, pans, glass bottles, a few knives, and the occasional dead chicken. On the floor were scattered tables filled with vials, mortars filled with stinky herbs, and enough books to fill a small public library. Half the walls were covered in bookcases, and the other half had astronomical charts and maps with red marks dotting many corners of the world.

Two familiar balding heads peeked out from opposite corners of the room behind the crowded tables. They were a pair of old men with thin, curious faces. They were Alyan and Utiradien, the ancient old fae who had cured me of a fever on our last visit. Their keen eyes swept over us before they settled on me. They scurried forward, tripping over much of their mess, and stopped on either side of me.

"Lady Miriam!"

"My Lady!"

Utiradien, being a bit on the blind side, groped for my arm and tested the limp muscle there. "Have you come to let us test your strength?"

Alyan circled us and looked me up and down. "We have heard you have gained great powers from the Sæ."

Muffy's eyes widened. "The Sæ exists?"

The curious old men paused and turned their attention to the young girl. Alyan arched an eyebrow. "You know of the ancient dragon waters, young human?"

Muffy shrank beneath their intense stares, but gave a weak nod. "Yes?" she squeaked.

Utiradien lifted his nose to the air and sniffed. "I smell the wonderful spice of the desert on you. Are you a wind user?"

"And a scholar all in one," I told them as I slipped away from their clutches and behind Muffy. I dropped my hands onto her shoulders so she couldn't slink off. "She also had questions that you might be able to answer."

They whipped their heads up to one another and their eyes lit up with glee. The pair swooped in and each grabbed an arm of Muffy's. She yelped as they lifted her off the floor and carried her to the far end of the room where they brushed away a pile of papers and books to set her in a chair. The pair slipped in front of her and smiled down at the pale young woman.

"Ask us anything," Alyan pleaded.

"Do not hesitate to inquire anything of us," Utiradien chimed in.

Muffy looked between them at us. Her eyes were large and her lower lip trembled. A sly grin slipped onto my lips as I grabbed Darda's hand and pulled her out of the room.

"Miriam!" Darda yelped as I paused and shut the door behind us. She freed herself from my grasp and spun around to frown at me. "Why did you have us leave her alone with them?"

I snorted. "You're the one who was saying they were sane, serene elders."

"I said no such thing!"

"You told me they were respected elders."

"As they are, but I do not see them as *responsible*, especially to such a meek child as Muff-Mufid."

"It's Muffy, and she can't keep using someone else as her crutch," I argued.

Darda's eyebrows crashed down. "She is merely young."

"Yeah, young glue. She sticks to that Father guy when he's around, or she sticks to us like everyone else has the plague." I folded my arms across my chest and pursed my lips. "Besides, if she wants to improve her magic skills she's going to have to find a little more confidence."

She pursed her lips as she looked past me at the door. "Perhaps you are correct."

"Of course, now how about we give her ten minutes alone? What harm can they do in that time?"

A scream erupted from behind the door. Darda and I whipped our heads toward each other before we both scrambled for the entrance. Together we flung open the door and stumbled inside.

The place was a mess, but it was like that before. What *was* different was that Muffy and the two strange old men lay on the ground in front of the chair. We hurried over. I didn't stop until I reached Muffy, but Darda knelt beside one of the two fae men.

Muffy lay on her stomach. I rolled her over into my arms and saw that her face was as pale as death. "Muffy! Muffy!" She groaned and shifted in my arms, but didn't wake up.

"They appear to have been knocked out from behind," Darda concluded as she studied a goose egg bump on the back of Utiradien's head.

Muffy's eyes fluttered open. They fell on me and widened. A sob escaped her lips and she wrapped her arms around me as she buried her face into my bosom. "Miriam! Thank the gods you're here!"

I pried us apart so I could down look into her tear-stained face. "What happened?"

She shook her head. "I-I don't know. T-they were asking me questions about Almukhafar when I saw this-"

"Quiet!" Darda hissed as her eyes swept over the room. She eased to a standing position as she drew a dagger from inside her dress. Her voice was so low I could barely here her words. "Something is here."

A shadow fell over me from behind. I was half-turned around when I saw a thin sword as black as night swipe at me. Darda darted between the danger and me, and I heard a clang of metal on metal. I lost my balance and twisted around to fall on my rear past where Muffy sat so that I faced our foe.

My eyes widened as I beheld a fae that was not a fae. It had the appearance of Durion, but its skin and clothes were as black as the darkest shadows. In place of his kind eyes, there were red coals. In the dim light of the aging day only this close of a proximity granted me the ability to see it.

Darda had unsheathed another of her daggers and blocked a downward death strike by the creature. My maidservant growled and flung her hand forward, forcing the creature backward a few steps. She stepped back so that she stood at my feet but still faced our foe with her daggers at the ready.

"What the hell is that thing?" I asked her.

Darda narrowed her eyes at the thing, and her words came out in a hiss. "A Sentinel."

CHAPTER 12

Muffy scrambled backward to sit even with me and pointed a shaking finger at the creature. "T-that's the thing that attacked them!"

I frowned and glanced back at the motionless creature as its red eyes stared with fire at Darda. "But I thought they were just supposed to protect the city! Why are they attacking-"

The creature's lips curled back in a snarl and it leapt ten feet into the air and over Darda. It grasped the hilt of its dark sword in both hands and brought the blade point-down upon Muffy and me. My eyes widened a split second before I leapt onto Muffy, wrapped my arms around her, and rolled us both out of the way. The creature crashed down on where we had just vacated. The force of the stab embedded the sword up to the hilt in the hard wood of the tree.

Darda swung both daggers down upon its body, but they sliced through its form without leaving so much as a wispy trail. The creature swung its arm back and knocked her in the jaw. She was thrown off her feet and crashed into a jumble of boxes some twenty feet away from us. The creature returned its red-eyed attention back to us.

"Time to go!" I yelped as I grabbed one of Muffy's hands and yanked her to her feet.

We raced to the door as the Sentinel grasped the hilt of its sword in both hands and yanked. The sword was pulled free and the creature sprinted after us. I threw a stream of water at the door and it wrapped around the handle. A quick tug back with my hand and the door flung open.

We flew through the entrance and I slammed it shut behind us. Muffy and I slid to a stop ten feet off and turned to the door. A shadow slipped through the crack beneath the door and reassembled itself into the dark Durion doppelganger.

I drew Muffy behind me and stretched my arms out in front of me. Water from my clothes slid down my arms and extended outward until they surrounded the Sentinel on both sides. I clapped my hands together, and the columns did the same, slamming their bodies into the shadow. Within the shifting water I glimpsed the Sentinel standing tall and unfazed.

I threw up my arms and my columns brushed against the ceiling. My water scraped two deep cuts into the tree and caused wood shavings to drift down on us like snow. "Oh come on! How the hell are we supposed to beat this thing?"

The creature, freed from my water, drew back its sword and rushed us. I held up my hands and created a water shield in front of us. The Sentinel cut through it like a hot knife through butter. I twisted to one side and saw too late that its weapon bore down on my young friend.

Muffy screamed and flung up her hands. A small tornado of air, though a larger one than what she'd shown Darda and me earlier, blew out from her palms and hit the

FOREST OF THE DRAGON

Sentinel square in the chest. The blast warped its body like a stone rippling the surface of a pond. The vibrations ran up and down its body, including its weapon, so that when the sword touched her it its solidness was gone so that it merely crawled across her arms.

Muffy yelped and jumped back. The Sentinel stumbled forward and raised its glowing red eyes to her. They narrowed as its form became solid again. The creature raised its sword above its head to bring down upon hers.

"Lakata!"

The Sentinel stopped and lowered its sword. Muffy and I regained the ability to breath, and looked to our left. Thorontur marched at the head of our friends and my dragon lord.

Xander hurried over to me and pursed his lips as he looked me over. "It seems I am unable to leave you alone until further notice."

I wrapped my arms around him and gave him a tight hug. "I'm getting a little tired of this constant danger, too." I glanced over at Thorontur as he stopped in front of the doppelganger of his son. I jabbed a finger at the creature. "That thing needs to be bottled and thrown into the ocean!"

Thorontur pursed his lips as he studied the Sentinel. "This is impossible. This Sentinel cannot be controlled by anyone save for my son."

"Have you had any problems with the Sentinels of late?" Xander asked him.

The king shook his head. "Never." He glanced at Muffy and me. "How did you provoke it?"

I snorted. "We didn't do anything." I glanced at Muffy who was being held up on her shaking legs by Tillit. "Muffy, tell him the first part."

Muffy shrank beneath the stares. "I-I was in there-" she pointed a shaking finger at the closed door, "-when this shadow came up behind the two nice men-"

"Alyan and Utiradien," I explained.

"-and it hit them on the back of the head with the hilt of its sword. Then I screamed and I-well, I think I fainted."

"That's when I found her on the ground and the thing attacked me," I continued. "I guess it figured we weren't using our heads and tried to chop them off, along with a couple of other body parts." I paused and furrowed my brow as I returned my attention to Muffy. "Speaking of losing things, how'd you make it go all ripply and lose its solidness? I couldn't even touch it."

She shook her head. "I-I don't know."

Thorontur turned to one of his guards. "Call back all the watchers and round up all the Sentinels. We cannot let another attack innocents." The guard bowed his head and hurried off to execute the orders. The fae king looked to Valo and her escort, and his eyes narrowed at them. "It is very strange that the Sentinels, so long a source of peace in my kingdom, would attack an innocent at your coming."

Xander frowned. "You are not the only victim of extraordinary circumstances, King Thorontur. The humans, too, were attacked by your ancient weapons, as Valo explained to you in the meeting." The king's body was still tense, but his expression softened. "And under these circumstances a truce would be a wise decision, at least until the true culprit of these terrible attacks is found."

Valo stepped toward him and bowed her head to the king. "Lord Xander is right, King Thorontur. We need to make an alliance before this hidden foe does any more terrible deeds."

The fae king pursed his lips. "Very well, but all I will agree to at the moment is a meeting, and I demand that it take place at the ancient site of Reuna Kivet. I will not have more humans within Metsan Keskella to upset the balance of our fae power."

Valo raised her head and gave a nod. "On behalf of my father I will agree to that."

FOREST OF THE DRAGON

Tillit swept his eyes over our company and furrowed his brow. "Where's Darda?"

My heart stopped. "Oh shit!" I rushed to the door, but it opened a foot before I reached it.

Darda stood on the other side clutching her head in one hand and a dagger in the other. She swept her eyes over the crowd before her gaze settled one me. "What have I missed?"

I snorted and gave her a tight hug. "Nothing special. Just another near-death experience."

She glanced over me and at Thorontur. "King Thorontur, Alyan and Utiradien have revived, but they may need some medical assistance."

Thorontur frowned. "They are our best physicians."

"Yes, but-" she stepped out of the way and revealed the pair.

They stood facing one another, and in their hands they each held a variety of weeds. The pair shook the weeds at one another, and the odor from those weeds wafted over we who stood outside the door and permeated the air.

"This is the best herb for head injury!" Alyan insisted.

Utiradien shook his head and his herbs. "No, no, no! Those are only useful in concocting headache pills!"

"But I have a headache!"

"That does not soothe the injury itself!"

"Nor does yours! You merely have some weeds pulled from the garden!"

"They are powerful herbs!"

"Weeds!"

"Herbs!"

Darda stepped outside the room and shut the door behind her. "I fear that their argument will not be quelled until a great many hours have passed."

Thorontur shook his head as he turned his attention to Valo. "I will meet with your father tonight, if that is convenient, or the next night, if he finds the date better suited to his schedule. For both days the hour will be sunset at the Reuna Kivet."

Valo bowed her head. "I will pass on your message, and return one as quickly as our swiftest horse can bring it."

"I would rather have my son bring me the message," Thorontur insisted.

Her face fell. "I don't know if my father will agree to your request."

"Consider it a gesture of good faith toward his commitment to this truce," he suggested. "For my part I will concede that you have a right to your ancestral lands. Of course, how much that entails will be worked out at a later date."

"Of course. Thank you, King Thorontur, and I will see that these messages are passed on to my father," Valo promised.

Thorontur returned her bow. "Now if you will excuse me, I must ensure that the other Sentinels are brought to the castle and properly controlled."

As he left I sidled up to Xander and lowered my voice to a whisper. "So how'd the meeting go?"

He pursed his lips as his eyes swept over Thorontur's leaving entourage. "Valo and I tried without success to convince Thorontur that a truce between groups, one in which neither side would trouble the other for a time, would be beneficial. Your trouble convinced him."

I snorted. "Well, at least something came out of my life-threatening fun." I wrinkled my nose as I thought back to that little adventure. "You know, there's one thing I don't get with this Sentinel stuff." He glanced down at me and arched an eyebrow. "When we were fighting that thing, I couldn't touch it with my water, but Muffy's tornado made it ripple and it couldn't hit her with its sword. How'd that happen?"

Xander sighed. "This is not a fact the fae wish to be broadcast, but wind is one of the Sentinel's few weaknesses.

The wind in a tornado reflects light on them from all angles so that they cannot hold their form. In trying to do so they lose strength and vanish, and are unable to immediately reconstitute their forms."

"That's a lot of science for magic."

"Science is often mistaken for magic, and so it may be the other way around."

Valo turned to us with a ghost of a smile on her lips. "We shall return home now."

Muffy's shoulders sagged and she sighed. "Thank goodness."

CHAPTER 13

We returned to the ruined city of Pimeys with one extra horse, that which belonged to Durion.

Mies himself met us at the edge of the encampment. Durion was with him, and under only one guard. "Well?" the human lord asked us.

Valo dismounted and hurried over to him to clasp his hands in hers. "We have an offer for truce, Father, that does not require us to stay in the camp, and for a meeting with the king at Reuna Kivet."

He arched an eyebrow. "I know you're a good diplomatic, my little naqia, but-" his eyes flickered to Xander, "-how did this happen? What convinced the fae king to a truce?"

"The fae have had their own problems," Xander told him as he stepped down off his horse. "One of their own ancient protectors in the city had to be subdued."

"A Sentinel?" Durion spoke up.

Xander nodded his head to him. "Yes, and it was your own Sentinel."

Durion started back and his eyes widened. "But that is not possible! I gave it no such orders!"

"Nonetheless, it attacked five people, nearly killing Miriam and Mufid before your father subdued it," he told him.

"You must accept this offer of a truce, Father, for both of our peoples," Valo pleaded with her parent.

He sighed, but gave a nod. "I accept, and I will have messengers-"

"The fae king requested that his son deliver the message," she added.

He frowned. "Does he think I'm that stupid to give away my only bargaining chip?"

Durion strode up to Mies and dropped to one knee before he bowed his head to the human lord. "Lord Mies, you have treated me well, but I must plead with you to be released from my promise to remain with you through this endeavor." He lifted his eyes to Mies and searched his face. "If it is my own shadow that has brought grief upon my people then I must go to them and right the wrong."

Mies pursed his lips, but gave a curt nod. "All right. I suppose you've proven yourself worthy enough of my respect to leave me, but-" he held up a finger, "-I expect you to return should your father renege on this truce. Do you understand?"

Durion nodded. "Yes, Lord Mies, and thank you."

Mies turned his head away, but he couldn't hide the hint of a smile on his lips. "Just go on with you, and tell your father we'll meet him at sunset today, but he'd better not be late."

Durion smiled and bowed his head before he hurried to his horse. The beast whinnied in glee at the sight of its master. He mounted and turned the side of the horse toward us. His eyes swept over our group, but his attention lingered on Valo.

"I thank you all for your hospitality, and may tonight bless both our peoples." He turned away and sped off into the woods.

Xander walked over to Mies and bowed. "Thorontur has instructed me on the basics of the ceremony, if you-"

Mies held up his hand and shook his head. "There's no need for that, dragon. If there's on thing my people remembered is how this whole mess could have been avoided. My ancestors and I have been training for this day for a very long time, and I'm glad I can be the one to finally put this ritual to use." He turned to face his guards and people, and raised his arms above his head. "Prepare your swords and shields! We go to the Reuna Kivet this evening!"

My jaw hit the ground before my feet did as I leapt off my horse and marched toward the front group of humans. "That's not how a truce-" Xander's heavy hand dropped onto my shoulder. I whipped my head up to him and pointed at Mies's back. "That's-"

"I will explain everything in due time," he promised before he looked to Darda who held the reins of her horse and mine. "For the moment I wish to speak with both of you alone."

"And me," Tillit spoke up.

I frowned up at Xander, but my attention was caught by another nearby scene. Father Darbat walked up to Muffy as she slipped down from her horse. He furrowed his brow as he studied her face. "You look pale."

She gave him a weak smile. "I'm fine. It was a long trip."

I winced and rubbed my posterior. "You're telling me. Any more riding and my ass is going to be rubbed so smooth that you'll be able to see your reflection on it."

Darbat arched an eyebrow at his young apprentice. "I see. Then let's attend to any preparations our lord might need for tonight." With that he led Muffy off to the depths of the keep.

With the humans off making merry, that left only Xander, Tillit, Darda, and me along the edges of the camp. Xander nodded at the forest. "Let us confer in the trees." Xander led our small group into the woods to a small clearing some fifty yards from the encampment. Once there he turned to Darda. "Do you still hold the chime?"

She nodded. "Yes, and no one is the wiser for it being down there."

Tillit looked her over and frowned. "Where exactly did you hide it?"

Her cheeks reddened as she glared at him. "That is none of your affair!"

He turned away and mumbled a few words. "And thank the gods for that. . ."

Darda clenched her hands into fists at her sides and stomped her foot. "You-! You piggish brute!"

Tillit winked at her. "Don't threaten me with a good name."

"I wish I could join in your mirth, my friends, but I believe the matter has grown very grave," Xander spoke up, squashing the cute squabbling between the pair. "If these machinations of the ancient forest creatures are not the work of a god than we may be dealing with a being outside our ability to overpower."

Tillit folded his arms in front of himself and shook his head. "It's definitely a god."

Xander arched an eyebrow. "Why do you say that with such certainty?"

He snorted. "Because if you three are here and there's trouble happening, then it's usually the worst possible scenario."

"And an unknown enemy wouldn't be worse?" I pointed out.

He shook his head. "Nope, because at this point you two-" he pointed at Xander and me, "-are probably capable of taking care of everything *but* a god."

A horn blew in the distance. Xander looked in the direction of the camp and pursed his lips. "It seems Mies has gathered his men and now begins the march toward Reuna Kivet."

I raised my hand. "Yeah, about that. Are we all headed to war, or is this some sort of a ceremony where his army gets dropped off halfway there and we pick them up on the way back?"

Xander smiled at me. "The rendezvous area is far enough through the forest that I will explain all to you on the way there."

I ran a hand through my hair and sighed. "My butt will never be the same. . ."

We saddled up and, from that vantage point, I glimpsed several long columns of men. All were armed, but some had only sharp hoes or old swords. At their head was Mies in a rusted suit of armor with an elegant sword sheath at his hip. On one side was his daughter, and on the other was Darbat. Sala and Muffy followed behind them, and at their backs were two dozen of the desert casters.

Mies drew out his sword, a shimmering reflection of steel much polished over countless generations, and raised the weapon above his head. "To Reuna Kivet!"

"To Reuna Kivet!" shouted his men.

With everyone at the ready we once more set out, this time into the northern part of the forest far above the fae and human cities. The Potami River where one of my uncles resided curved around the northern part of the forest before it went south to drain into the ocean along the western coast of the continent just north of the desert. It was a natural border between the lands ruled by Xander and those administrated by King Thorontur.

FOREST OF THE DRAGON

Along the way I heard the snapping voice of Darbat. "I told you to remove that! It is not part of the customary attire for this ceremony!"

"But it's in my shirt," Muffy argued.

I glanced over my shoulder at the pair. Muffy clutched the front of her shirt with one hand and the reins in the other.

Darbat glared at the hand that held the shirt and thrust his hand out to her. "Give it to me."

"W-what if I was to put it in the book?" she suggested.

His eyebrows crashed down. "You would mar the pages of a book for your own selfishness?"

"Then my pocket," she persisted as she drew a frayed rope from around her neck and tucked the item into her pocket. "No one can see it there."

Darbat pursed his lips, but looked ahead. "Make sure they-" he noticed my spying on them and his frown deepened. "Is there something you wanted, dragon Maiden?" I shook my head and returned my gaze to the front.

The trees were a thick mess that bogged down our march, but no one hacked a limb or suggested we blow up the whole thing. We were forced off our horses and into a narrow trail that was surrounded on all sides, and sometimes over our heads, by a dense bush of thorns. Their thick branches full of sharp teeth blocked out the sun and encased us in a cavern of darkness with only a light at the end to give hope.

I bumped against Xander as we walked side-by-side through the brambles. "Does anybody have a match?" I mumbled.

"Injuring a plant on the road to Reuna Kivet is forbidden," Xander told me.

I leaned away from the thorns and eyed them with even greater suspicion than before. "Why? Are they veggies carnivores?"

He shook his head. "I cannot be sure. The ritual of human and fae meeting at Reuna Kivet for a truce is more ancient than even my dragon lineage. I would be surprised if anyone who still lives knows the reason for the rule."

We continued through another few miles through the thicket before the path opened. The trees gave way before a large plain of grass that gently sloped upward to a short hill. The hill was punctuated by ten-foot wide steppes every fifteen feet. Wide stones, some ten feet across and a half a foot thick, led up to the flat top. Atop the hill stood a ring of stones like the Henge of my old world.

In such a wide space everyone parted company, especially as the walk through the thorns had left the whole company sweaty and smelly. Mies handed off his horse to his men and walked up the stone steps with his men at his back. At each level the columns parted ways until that steppe was full, and they continued that way until the soldiers reached the top steppe. That location ended some thirty feet below the crest of the hill.

Mies, with Valo, Darbat, and Muffy, continued to the top. My group, led by Xander, followed them to the highest height. The ring of stones towered some fifteen feet above our heads. Around their bases were flat stones sunken into the grass-covered ground. In the center of the stones was a small pool of water with a stone bench on our side and the one opposite us. The source of the water originated from within the pool as water bubbled from a small fountain in the center.

I paused at the top step and turned in a circle to see the incredible view. The forest stretched into the distance all around us. To the far north some miles off was a cut in the trees that signified the running waters of the Potami River. In the northeast stood a few other, smaller hills clumped together. To the southwest stood the largest of the forest trees, and in them somewhere resided the fae. To the southeast were the blackened ruins of Pimeys. A few whiffs of smoke like tiny strings signified campfires.

Mies took a seat on the bench and faced the opposite one. The setting sun lay to our left. At our backs the troops shifted from one tired foot to the other. I couldn't blame them. The march had taken a good three hours, most of it through bramble. The day was nearly spent, and so was I as my stomach growled at me.

Darda stood at my side and gave me a disapproving look. I sheepishly smiled and shrugged. "It's got a mind of it's own."

Movement caught my eye so that I took a step forward and stretched my neck to see down the hill in front of us. A long line of fae soldiers, four abreast, marched out of the woods and up the wide stone steps. They were dressed in their finest silver armor polished until the setting sun reflected off their surfaces like shooting stars.

At their lead was King Thorontur, and at his side was his son. Their armor was silver covered in a fine layer of gold that made them glisten like the sun as they walked up the steps. Directly behind the pair walked Alyan and Utiradien with their heads wrapped in white bandages, and at their backs were fae who wore long green robes that trailed the ground. The soldiers followed and filled the steppes up the hill, and still the line went down the steps and disappeared into the trees.

A different movement in those trees made me squint. My blood froze as I noticed the shadowy figures of hundreds of Sentinels, each as armed as their non-shadow counterparts.

I leaned toward Xander and lowered my voice to a whisper. "Tell me again why both sides have to bring all their guys?"

"So that any qualms will be settled here with words or-" his eyes flickered to the tree line where the fae army disappeared, "-with force. That is why this place is called the

Reuna Kivet, the Edge Stones. Both sides are on the edge of war or peace, and if it should be war than the matter will be decided with a single battle far away from the people."

"So what happened the last time they had a war?" I wondered.

Xander pursed his lips. "The arguments started over land rights between the hunting fae and the farming humans, and those arguments too quickly escalated into battle for a truce to be called."

I looked up at the large stone to my right and pursed my lips. "So this is a burial ground, too?"

"Yes. Each of the armies walks upon the fields of their dead as a reminder of that dangerous path should their leaders be tempted to choose war over truce."

Thorontur, Durion, and the two crazy fae reached the top of the hill where the king took a seat on the bench opposite Mies. They bowed their heads as the sun shone its weakening light on their tense faces.

The armies were at the ready, the leaders were at the stones, and I was chomping at the bit to get this thing done with.

It turns out I should have been enjoying that short reprieve.

CHAPTER 14

Darbat stepped between them and raised his arms to the sky. "Let the session of the High Lords commence, and may the god who grows the grass bless them and give them guidance. So says the humans."

Both Alyan and Utiradien stepped forward. They stopped and glared at one another.

"It is my duty to officiate the opening," Alyan insisted.

Utiradien shook his head. "No, it is mine."

"Your head was more damaged than we thought. It is my duty."

"Your memory was affected. It is my duty."

Mies sat stiffly on his bench, but his shoulders shook from silent laughter. A little snort escaped his lips. His daughter set a hand on his shoulder so that he contained himself again.

The fae king looked over his shoulder and glared at the pair. "Alyan. Utiradien," Thorontur snapped.

"The king calls me," Alyan asserted.

"No, he calls *me*," Utiradien argued.

There was a brief shoving match with their elbows before the near-blind Utiradien stepped back. Alyan, still in the game of bone-knob warfare, lost his balance and stumbled sideways to the far edge of the henge.

Utiradien hurried forward and stood opposite Darbat where he raised his arms as the father had done. "Let the session of the High Lords commence, and may the god who grows the grass bless them and give them guidance. So says the fae."

Mies set one arm on his leg and leaned forward to size up the fae king. "I am Mies, lord of the humans of Pimeys."

Thorontur bowed his head. "I am Thorontur the Fourth, ruler of the forest of Virea Metsa, southern gatekeeper to the lands of Alexandria, and High King among fae."

Mies couldn't stifle a laugh. "I hope this truce lasts as long as your name. Then my daughter won't have to worry about a thing."

Thorontur narrowed his eyes at the human. "This is strange. I can see little resemblance in your manners compared to the high manners of your daughter."

"Father," Durion hissed.

Mies frowned. "What's that supposed to mean?"

"Father," Valo whispered.

"My words mean what they mean," Thorontur challenged him.

Mies leapt to his feet and glared at his opponent. "Keep your words. I'll have this-" he drew his sword and stepped to the side, "-and your apology."

"Lord Mies, King Thorontur," Xander scolded the pair.

Thorontur unsheathed his sword and stepped to the side to confront Mies. "Lord Xander, for once I must request that you remain apart from this fight."

Valo rushed over to her father and grabbed one of his arms. "Father, you mustn't!"

He shrugged her off and shook his head as he kept his eyes on Thorontur. "This is something I've been practicing for my entire life, Valo. Don't get in the way."

"Father, you must set aside your animosity for the humans and return to your seat," Durion pleaded.

"Do not interfere," Thorontur ordered his son as he eased toward his foe. "If the human wishes to lose in this fashion than we shall allow it."

Xander stood near by me. I slipped over to him and elbowed him gently in the side. He glanced down at me, and I gave him a wink before I spoke in a low voice. "I think it's time you showed them what a dragon can do."

A sly smile slipped onto his lips as he bowed his head. "If that is what my Maiden wishes."

I glanced over my shoulder at the unprepared human army. "Me, and a whole bunch of other people."

Xander straightened to his full height and strode up to the pair of fighters so that he stood between them and slightly to the side. They paused and glared at his intrusion.

"Lord Xander, please step aside!" Thorontur commanded him.

"Move!" Mies hissed.

Xander unfurled his wings, and their greenish-blue hue glowed in the dim light of the sun. They stretched across the full length of the hilltop and curled around our two groups so that everyone not on the top was blind to all but his wings.

Muffy clasped her hands against her chest and her fingers dug into her shirt, but her eyes stared in wonder at the shimmering light. "By all the gods. . ." she whispered.

Sala had a wide smile on his lips as he swept his eyes over Xander's beauty. "Very impressive, even for a dragon lord."

The human lord lowered his weapon and gawked at the size of the wings, but the fae king looked to Xander and frowned. "I cannot stress enough to what danger you allow yourself to become involved in by-" Xander's gaze fell on the fae king, and at their bright green glow Thorontur started back. The fae king's own eyes widened and his mouth dropped open. "Surely. . .surely you have not achieved the tenth generation," he whispered.

"Whether I have or not, I will use all my powers to ensure that both of you hear one another out so that your peoples have a chance to live in peace," Xander promised.

I stepped closer and held up one hand. A small ball of water appeared and swirled over my palm. "Ditto."

Darda drew out her daggers and slipped up beside me. "As will I."

Tillit hitched up his pants and joined me by my side. "I'm in."

"Father, you must be more reasonable," Valo pleaded with her parent.

Mies pursed his lips, but sheathed his sword. "I. . .I suppose I was a bit hasty."

"Father," Durion scolded his own parent.

Thorontur frowned, but also put away his weapon. "As you wish, Lord Xander, but I fail to see how an alliance with these humans-" he gestured down the hill where Xander's wings hid the human army, "-will be of any use against our shared enemy."

"A helping hand is a hand worth having," Darda mused.

Xander smiled at her. "A saying my mother was very fond of-"

"And for good reason," Darda added.

FOREST OF THE DRAGON

He bowed his head. "You are correct again." He returned his attention to the leaders. "Regardless of past quarrels, the future is covered by the cloud of this unknown attacker. Together you may be able to overcome their wiles, but apart you will surely both fail."

I heard a soft snap of fingers behind me, but before I could turn around a violent tremor struck. The stones that towered above us rocked from side to side, and the water in the pool sloshed back and forth so violently that its spray soaked us.

I clutched onto Darda and whipped my head up to Durion as he tried to stay upright. "Please tell me that's just a normal earthquake!"

He stumbled into one of the stones and shook his head. "We have no earthquakes."

Xander furled his wings so that we were given a full view of the forest. A cloud of dust arose in the northeast where the smaller hills were located. Through the thick clouds I glimpsed movement, big movement.

Both armies started back as a large form flew out of the top of the dust cloud and spread its wings high in the air. The wings were made of leaves so thin that light would have shone threw them had they not been piled layer upon layer on top of a structure of hollow branches. Those branches made up the bones and were connected to the thick, trunk-like brown body of a creature that resembled a butterfly. Its head was round and antenna poked out from the top. The beast's wings stretched twenty feet on either side, and from head to the end of its abdomen was another thirty feet. Its eyes were hard rocks like those of the taimet.

The size wasn't the biggest issue, it was the numbers. Three of the creature emerged from the dust, and as the cloud settled I saw that the hills had disappeared, or rather, the beasts that flew above the area *were* the hills. Now freed from their stone imprisonment, the creatures let loose with a high-pitched, shrill call that made me clap my hands over my ears.

Thorontur gaped at the green-and-brown monsters, and a few strangled words were whispered from his lips. "By all the gods. . ."

"What are those, Father?" Durion asked him.

The fae king swallowed the lump in his throat and looked to Xander. My own dragon lord's narrowed eyes were fixed on the beasts. "Lord Xander, they are-"

"-lentaja," Xander finished for him. I was surprised to hear anger in his voice.

"What's a lentaja?" I spoke up.

"They are called 'slayers of air' because they were the creatures the fae used against my ancestors to protect the forest when the dragons attempted to conquer the woods," Xander explained.

I snorted. "Your ancestors got beaten by a bunch of butterflies?"

One of the butterflies hovered in front of its two compatriots. It turned slightly to the side and thrust its wings forward in a hard flap. The flap created a wind that blasted through the trees and slammed them into the ground. The single flap left a path of devastation fifty yards wide and a half mile long. The creator of that leveling turned back so it faced us.

I swallowed the lump in my throat and whipped my head to Thorontur. "Please tell me there's no more ancient, near-mythical monsters leftover from these wars."

His gaze lay on the devastation as he pursed his lips. "No, and these are the most terrible of the three. Even my ancestors could barely contain their power so that they did not turn on those who commanded them."

"But you can control these things, right?" Mies asked the fae king.

Thorontur shook his head. "The power I hold is much weaker than those of my ancestors. I doubt I have the strength to even catch its attention."

I pointed a finger at the fae king. "You need to start burying these things a little deeper." I then turned my attention to Xander who continued to glare at the monsters. I swore the leader of the flock stared back at him. "Did your ancestors ever defeat one of these things?"

"Many died trying, though with enough dragons they were able to burn them to cinders," he revealed.

"Do you think you've got enough spark in you for that?" I asked him.

He shook his head. "I do not know."

Muffy stepped forward and furrowed her brow as she studied the beasts. "What are they waiting for?"

"For their masters to command them," Thorontur replied.

The lead lentaja let loose another high-pitched screech before it raced toward us, leaving its two brethren behind. Each flap of its wings pushed down on the canopy of trees and violently shook the branches so that many leaves were lost.

"Duck down!" the fae king yelled.

We dove for the ground, and the soldiers on both sides of the hill copied us. Some of the slower soldiers were struck by the gust of wind as the lentaja flew over us. They were pulled off their feet and landed on their compatriots two steppes lower then where they started.

We scurried to our feet and watched the lentaja make a u-turn and come back at us.

"Does anybody have any idea how we can all not die?" I asked my compatriots. Xander pursed his lips and took a step forward as he unfurled his wings. I grabbed his arm and looked up into his face. "What are you doing? That thing could crush you with one wing!"

He looked down at me and smiled. "Then I leave Alexandria in good hands."

CHAPTER 15

Xander pulled out of my grasp and leapt into the sky. I tried to catch his foot, but Darda grabbed my arms and pulled me back. I thrashed in her hold and whipped my head around to glare at her. "What are you doing? We have to stop him!"

"The defeat of his ancestors has left a stain on his family for many years," she pointed out as her eyes followed his ascent. "We must let him avenge them."

Tillit strode up to us with a grin on his lips and a large paper cannon in his arms. "He didn't say we couldn't help, though."

My eyes widened as I glimpsed the cannon. "Are you seriously going to shoot those things off here?"

Darda glared at him. "Shoot what off?"

Tillit shouldered the cannon and winked at her. "You'll see."

"No, I will not!" Darda insisted as she lunged for the cannon. Tillit stepped aside, but she twisted around and grabbed one side while he clutched onto the other. "You will not use artillery while Xander is in the skies!"

"I can't use Boreas, so these vampiri de hârtie will have to work!" Tillit insisted.

Darda's mouth dropped open. "You have *what* in this cannon?"

Tillit took advantage of her shock and yanked the cannon from her grasp. "They're trained," he defended himself.

Muffy furrowed her brow. "But vampiri de hârtie are impossible to train."

Darda's eye twitched before she lunged at Tillit. "Give that to me!"

"Guys!" I shouted as I pointed up at the sky. "Xander!"

Xander had reached the same height of the lentaja and hovered above us. His wings expanded as his body took the shape of his full dragon form. In a few seconds my handsome dragon lord was gone, and in his place was the majestic dragon beast, the fulfillment of nine generations of dragons.

The lentaja screeched and charged at him. Xander snapped at his opponent and met the creature halfway so that they clashed a little to the left of the hill. The lentaja whipped up a tornado with its wings and lobbed the focused storm at Xander. He dodged the blow and swung in a circle so that his long tail struck the lentaja in the side. The butterfly screeched as it flew backward and crashed down in the woods at the bottom of the hill. Xander leaned back his head and released a mighty roar.

"By the gods. . ." Thorontur murmured.

I shook my head. "Nope, by Xander, and some goop."

FOREST OF THE DRAGON

The lentaja raised its head from the broken trees and let off a low, garbled scream that echoed across the plain. The other two lentaja heard the call of their brethren and flew at Xander. He turned around as they both unleashed tornadoes. The spinning winds slammed into him and tore at his wings, tattering the thin leather. Xander roared as he fell onto the same side of the hill as his fallen foe, but he remained on the slope.

The lentaja screeched in glee as their comrade stood and stretched out its wings. Parts of the wings were tattered, but it flexed its wings and took off into the air. The shadows of the three lentaja now loomed above us, and my dragon lord lay unconscious on the ground.

A gust of wind blew past me and upward to the lentaja. The single flicker of air forced them to adjust their wing speed and floated them apart just slightly.

I whipped my head to Darbat and his minions. "Wind! Blow those things out of the sky!"

"We will handle our own creations!" Thorontur insisted as he looked to Alyan and Utiradien. "Pull them to the ground!"

Mies frowned at him. "We won't be left out of any fight! Darbat!" He turned to his priest and jabbed a finger at the two lentaja. "Take those things down!"

The priests of both parties gathered together and clasped their hands in front of themselves. Green light came from the fae while the humans showed yellow from their hands.

Tillit dropped to one knee on the ground and set his bag before him. He tucked the cannon away into the infinite space within the satchel before he began a rummage through the other contents. "What I wouldn't do for a witch about now. . ." he mumbled as his eyes flickered to Darda. "You don't happen-" Her glare made him resume his digging in his bag. "Right. Not a good time."

As Tillit searched the priests on both sides held up their glowing hands. Darbat stood before his group, while Alyan and Utiradien stood before theirs. The light of the priests shot from their hands and into the palms of their respective leaders. Darbat took the light and molded his into a swirling ball of wind, while Alyan and Utiradien slammed their palms onto the ground.

The earth shook and the air quivered as the two powers erupted into being. A great tangling vines shot up from the earth and stretched upward into the sky to wrap around the lentaja while Darbat threw his ball into the air. The ball burst into dozens of small, stringy tornadoes that swirled around the beasts. Darbat raised one open hand to the air and clamped his fingers shut into a fist.

The yellow magic slammed into the green one that encompassed the lentaja. There was a burst of yellow-green light that resembled puke before a shock wave blew over us. I tumbled backward head over heels and rolled over the gentle slope of the hill. The world spun around me for a few seconds as I clawed at air and dirt. A hand caught me and drew me against a warm chest.

I looked up into the battered and dirty face of my once-more-human dragon lord. Xander still had his wings out, and his hands were more claws than fingers. His breathing was rough as he raised his eyes to the top of the hill some fifty feet above us.

I followed his gaze and watched in horror as the magics combined and transformed into a tornado of immense size. The vines were absorbed into the wind and the wind into the vines so that they made a whip that thrashed out at anything and everything. The green whips lashed out at the lentaja and struck them from the sky. The screams of the creatures were barely heard above the roar of the winds as they toppled into the woods, breaking tree and bush on their landing. They remained still as the vines cracked above their heads.

FOREST OF THE DRAGON

Other spinning vines slammed into the stones and toppled many of them. One of those stones slipped off the top of two others and slid down the hill toward us. Xander clenched his teeth and opened his wings out behind him. The wind from the magics yanked us off the ground and into the air. We got a great view of the carnage as our friends and companions ducked and dove for cover. The winds stretched out into the woods and grabbed the foliage, wrenching bush and tree alike from the ground and drawing them up into its insatiable mouth.

Xander landed us beside one of the upright stones just as Mies threw himself onto the ground as a bush passed overhead. He lifted his head and found Darbat near him in the same position. "Make this wind stop!"

Darbat shook his head. "I can't! The fae magic is controlling it!"

"Not our magic!" Alyan and Utiradien yelled together as they lay on their bellies beside the pool.

Alyan pointed a finger at Darbat. "It is *you* who is in the wrong!"

"Your magic interferes with us controlling our own!" Utiradien added.

"Tillit!" I heard Darda scream.

I looked in their direction and watched Tillit grab hold of the strap of his satchel as the wind tried to carry it off. He dug his feet into the ground, but the wind dragged his heels across the soft dirt until his toes hit the stone sides of the pool. Tillit fell face-first into the water and his satchel was taken up into the tornado. The flap was opened wide and the Boreas, the wind that protected his bag, blew out and combined with the spinning gusts.

The tornado sucked in the new wind like a child with candy. Its size increased two-fold so that the illuminated behemoth cast a shadow over us. The quick wind traveled over the pool and sucked up all the water, revealing a wet Tillit. The water mixed with the earth and leaves and changed the yellow-green glow to an ugly brown. The winds tossed out mud balls that slapped against the stones and ground. Xander grabbed the back of my head and shoved both of us down as the balls spit over our heads.

Movement caught my eye and forced my gaze up. Sala stood amid the muck with a smile on his face and his eyes wide as he watched the tornado spin violently before him. The mucky brown exterior flung mud everywhere, and some of that mud smacked the face of Sala. The force of the blow pulled him off his feet and flung him back ten feet where he landed hard on his back. I rose to my feet to go to him, but Xander leapt up and grabbed my shoulders.

"Sala!" Muffy yelled. She tried to sprint forward, but Father Darbat caught her.

"Stay back, you fool!" Darbat snapped at her.

Sala stumbled to his feet and wiped the mud from his face. My heart skipped a beat as he wiped his eyes clean and revealed their glowing green color. The spot where the mud had struck him was as red as a cherry and slightly swollen.

Though the wind battered our ears, I clearly heard his voice over the gale. "I'm not having fun anymore."

CHAPTER 16

Sala stretched one arm over his hand and splayed his fingers apart. The earth trembled so violently that only Xander's hands on my shoulders kept me from falling. Many of the others fell to their knees or onto their rears.

Large fissures opened in the earth and the same forest behemoths from the human camp climbed out of the holes. The wind tore at their foliage and battered their bark hides. Some of the smaller birds flew into the air only to be torn apart by the tornado. The grounded animals bellowed before they charged the trunk of the gale. The first creatures were taken up by the winds and tossed out.

One of the rhino-like things flew straight at us. Xander grabbed me by the shoulders and threw us both to the ground so that his body covered me. The rhino sailed over us and slammed into a tree. The tree shattered and the beast kept flying, but the second tree caught it and dropped the creature to the ground.

The second wave of beasts rushed the base of the cyclone and interfered with its spinning winds. The wind slowed with each rotation and in a minute the tornado had died to nothing. A soft mist of dust fell around us like brown snow, but that, too, settled. With the dying of the winds the lentaja rose from their fallen places and once more hovered in the sky.

We were worse than back to square one. The armies were beaten and battered by the winds, rocks, brush and limbs the tornado had thrown up. The fae were the better off, however, because many of the humans were laid low by the dust kicked up by the winds. They sneezed and coughed, and there were several dozen who lay on their backs and merely groaned.

We on the top of the hill climbed to our feet and looked to our savior. Sala turned to us, and as he did his features changed in a shimmer of light. His hair lengthened to cascade over his back like the fae, and his skin transformed to a smooth alabaster.

"Luoja!" Thorontur gasped before he dropped to his knees and bowed his head.

Durion stared at his prostrate father with wide eyes. "Luoja? He is real?"

"Who the heck is Luoja?" I spoke up.

"Lord Luoja is the Creator, the Lord of the Forest," Durion told me as he stared in awe at the god. "It was he who created Viridi Silva and invited humans and fae to live among its trees."

Sala grinned and bowed low to us. "The one and only."

Mies's jaw dropped open. "A god of the woods?" He whipped his head to Father Darbat. "Is what he says is true?" Darbat's jaw moved up and down, but no sound came out.

"There. . .there are a few stories about a god in the trees," Muffy spoke up.

Mies returned his attention to the god and a sly smile slipped onto his lips. "Well I'll be. . ."

Thorontur bowed his head a little lower before the young god. "Lord Luoja, why have you not walked among us and blessed us with your presence for so long?"

Sala wrinkled his nose. "That old name. I much prefer the name I gave myself to join the humans. 'Sala' has such a nice ring to it, like a little sing-song."

Thorontur raised his head a little and pursed his lips. "My Lord, we are your loyal faithful and you make your appearance during our hour of need, do you not?"

He sighed and forlornly shook his head. "I do not. The fae have always been too uptight to have fun with. The humans, however-" his eyes flickered to Mies's group and a smile slipped onto his lips, "-are much more interesting. They remember how to have fun."

Mies hurried forward and dropped to one knee before the giant stalk. He opened his arms to the god and looked up at him. "My Lord, I beseech you on behalf of my people to help us in our fight against these fae."

"No god would side with your wickedness!" Thorontur argued.

Mies whipped his head to the fae and scowled at him. "No decent person, god or human, would align themselves with *you*."

"Quiet!" the god boomed. The earth quaked beneath our feet and the huge stone pillars rocked from side-to-side. He relaxed his shoulders and cleared his throat. "As I was going to say, I don't play favorites. I thought maybe bringing you two together would mean more fun for me, but I see that you can't get along at all. That means you *both* have to leave."

Thorontur shook his head. "I do not understand, My Lord. Leave where?"

Sala looked up and raised his hands to the canopy. "This forest."

Thorontur's mouth dropped open. "But this is our home! We cannot leave!"

Sala jabbed a finger at the trees ruined by the beast thrown by the tornado. "I didn't create this forest for your two species to destroy it. Even your own magics don't get along, so since I can't trust you two to play nice then you have to leave."

"Please give us a second chance!" Thorontur pleaded.

The god sneered at him. "This *was* your second chance. Your kinds failed to get along those few short years ago when I cursed the human home so they wouldn't come back, and even after doing that neither of you learned anything from it."

Mies stepped forward. "But that was a long time ago in our years. Maybe if we-"

"No," Sala refused as he pointed up at the sun. "You have three sunsets to move everyone out of the forest, otherwise my beasts will help you."

"But where will we go, My Lord?" Thorontur asked him.

Sala shrugged. "Wherever you wish, though-" he chuckled. Nobody laughed with him. "-I recommend far from humans."

Xander stepped forward and met the indifferent gaze of the god with his own unblinking one. "You know I was summoned here by King Thorontur to assist in this affair, but what you do not know is Crates of the Mallus Library has entrusted me with another task."

Sala sneered at him. "That old goat? What does he want?"

"He wishes for you to return to your world."

Sala leaned his head back and loosed a loud laugh. "Really? And what army is he going to use against me? These?" He swept one arm over the unsteady armies of the fae and humans. "They couldn't even do anything against my lentaja. What do you have that-" He froze and his eyes widened. Sala whipped his head to Darda and narrowed his eyes. "You have it, don't you? That's why you put off such a horrible aura."

Tillit snorted. "No, that's the way she usually is." Darda glared daggers at him

Xander nodded. "If you mean the Theos Chime, then yes, that is in our possession."

The god opened his arms and grinned at Xander. "All right, hit me with it, but they-" he jerked his head toward the , "-won't be too happy about me being gone. I can pretty much guarantee that without me controlling them there won't be a forest left for anyone."

"Might I suggest an alternative?" Xander mused.

Sala lowered his arms and arched an eyebrow. "What kind of alternative?"

"That we play a game."

A smile slipped onto Sala's lips. "I'm listening."

"The humans, fae, and my friends against you for ownership of the forest," Xander proposed.

The god frowned. "But I can get that now and you have no way to win."

A sly smile slipped onto my lips as I saw Xander's plan. I stepped forward to stand beside my dragon lord. "What are you afraid of?" I challenged him.

Sala scoffed. "I fear nothing."

"Then why hesitate? It's a guaranteed win for you, and you get to prove us wrong about these guys-" I thrust a thumb over my shoulder at Mies and Thorontur. "*We* still think they might be able to work together and beat your butt at any game."

Sala rubbed his chin with one hand, but couldn't hide a ghost of a smile. He dropped his hand and shrugged. "Why not? It's custom for the one offering to accept whatever games the offered suggests, so I get to choose the games."

Xander stepped aside and gestured to the people who lay wounded on the ground. "Might we first treat our wounded?"

Sala shrugged. "All right. You ten-" he swept his hand over the main four humans, the two fae, and our group of four, "-and you ten alone will come back here at midnight tonight and I'll show you what I have in store for you, but be punctual. I don't like to wait."

He snapped his fingers and a crack appeared three feet in front of him. The crack raced around him in a circle until it met itself where some of the earth then fell away to reveal that he stood on a platform over a deep hole. Sala gave us a wink before the platform lowered into the earth like an elevator.

Xander hurried up to the hole and looked down. I wasn't far behind, and together we stared into the deep elevator shaft. The hole was illuminated by the god's light and we could see it went down for what looked to be a hundred yards before his movement stopped. His light expanded outward beyond the rim of the platform. He stepped off and walked out of sight. There was a groan from around the hole. Xander and I jumped back as tree roots slithered out from all sides of the opening and closed the hole by intertwining with one another until there wasn't even a sliver of a view down the shaft.

I glanced up at Xander and pursed my lips. "'Within the cradle, slumbers thee, if one is able, come conquer me.'"

Xander nodded. "I was thinking of the same rhyme."

"You sure it wasn't a good idea to use the Chime on him?"

Xander half-turned to face our company and sighed. "No."

FOREST OF THE DRAGON

CHAPTER 17

I followed his gaze and beheld devastation. A few of the stones were toppled and most of the trees outside the ring were battered or outright broken. The heavy mist of dust was gone, but its pungent odor of damp forest air lingered over the area.

The fae were a little bruised, but otherwise they stood on their feet. The humans weren't so lucky. Most of the warriors lay on the ground sneezing and coughing. Some were completely unconscious as their comrades tried to awaken them.

One of those struck hardest by the mist was Valo. She lay on the ground near one of the large stones. Her father rushed to her side and shook her shoulders while Father Darbat and Muffy stood off to the side.

"Valo! My little naqia! Please wake up!" Mies pleaded. He whipped his head up to his priest. "Do something!"

Darbat shook his head. "I wouldn't know where to start, My Lord."

Durion hurried over and knelt at Valo's head. Her father looked at him with pleading eyes. "Can you help her?"

Durion lay his hand over her forehead and studied her scrunched up face. "I believe so. She appears to have been struck by a very strong Metsä Nenä, no doubt from the mist."

"And that's what?" Mies asked him.

"It is what has been making your people sick, but we fae have the cure," Durion explained to him. He raised his eyes and looked out over the fallen men. "While I provided ingredients to your doctors, there is not enough for this many of the strong cases. These men must be taken to Metsan Keskella to be properly treated."

Fae King Thorontur's royal demeanor was marred when his mouth dropped open. "What are you suggesting, my son? That with our defensive walls now complete we would allow a foreign army into them?"

"The humans have neither the beds nor the expertise to deal with so many ill," Durion argued.

Thorontur shook his head. "No, I will not allow it. They may remain here and be treated by their own while we attend to ours."

"We do not know what games this god has in store for us, so it would be wise to move everyone from this area," Durion insisted.

"Then the humans may move their own," Thorontur countered. He half-turned away from his son and toward his soldiers, but paused when he saw his son didn't move from the woman's side. "Leave the human to her own, my son."

Durion stood and turned to face his father. "I am sorry, Father, but this once I cannot follow your commands. These people need our help as we need theirs."

Thorontur's eyebrows crashed down. "Then you would help our enemy over your own people?"

"Show them goodness and be shown in kind," Darda spoke up.

Thorontur turned his ire on her. "Kindness? Goodness? Their foolishness has wrought doom upon my people and turned my own son-" he waved a hand at Durion, "-against me!"

"That's enough." All eyes fell on Mies where he remained by his daughter's side. His hands grasped one of hers, and a few tears pooled in his eyes as he looked upon her shut eyes. Her chest moved up and down, and harsh breaths escaped her parted lips. He clenched his teeth and whipped his head around to look up at Thorontur. "I won't agree to your terms, but we can't fight about that right now! Not when there's something bigger to deal with!"

"He is correct," Xander spoke up as he stepped forward. "A god is a greater danger to everyone than any past squabbles."

I raised my hand. "I'll third that motion."

Thorontur glared at Xander. "Lord Xander, you are hardly a voice of reason in all of this. What was this 'chime' you mentioned to Lord Luoja that would have granted us safety from his ire?"

"Safety from the god, perhaps, but not from them," Xander countered as he gestured to the lentaja that still hovered close by the hillside. "We have no way to control them on our own, so to release them from his control might have placed us in a worse position than the one in which we find ourselves."

Durion lifted Valo into his arms and turned to his father. "For the sake of both our people, Father, we must *all* be at our full strength."

The fae king pursed his lips, but turned to his side of the hill where his men gathered enough strength to stand before him. "We will assist the humans in their travel to Metsan where they will be our guests until their health improves. Each fae help those most ill and return for the rest." He looked to Alyan and Utiradien. "Alert the city to expect our guests and have beds at the ready along with the cure for Metsä Nenä." They bowed their heads and hurried down the hill to where a few horses had been rounded up. Thorontur turned his head to one side so that he looked at his son with one eye. "I hope we do not come to regret this hospitality."

The fae king looked away and strode off down the hill. Durion's face fell and his shoulders slumped. He looked down into the pale face of Valo and pursed his lips.

Xander walked up to him and set a hand on his shoulder. "Come. Let us return to Metsan." Durion nodded, and together with Mies close behind they followed Thorontur.

I took a step forward to catch up, but Darda's voice made me pause and look to my left. "How could you have such a thing in your satchel?" she snapped at Tillit.

Tillit knelt on the ground with his bag before him. He had the flap in one hand and his hand buried deep in the endless interior of his bag. His face was scrunched up as he pushed down on the bag like he was doing CPR. "It's. Helped. Before," he grunted with each push.

"But to have a windstorm, of all things! And a cannon of those dreadful vampiri de hârtie!" she scolded him.

Tillit yanked out his hand and a gust of wind followed. He slapped the flap over the mouth and tied it closed before he fell back on his posterior and sighed. "All fixed."

Darda looked at him in horror. "Fixed? *Fixed?* How can you possibly believe that that-that-" she waved her hand at his satchel, "-that *bag* is capable of holding such horrible things for very long?"

Tillit stood and drew the strap of his satchel across his ample chest. "Because this was a gift from the Blesk, and if it's one thing they know how to do is make something as proof against the elements as possible."

I blinked at him. "The who?"

Tillit opened his mouth, but a quiet voice spoke up first. "They're a people located in the far northeast of the continent in the cold valleys of Temno where the sun rarely shines, even in summer." We all glanced over to Muffy who was the source of the educational information.

Tillit smiled at her. "You sound like you read a lot of books."

Muffy shrank back, but nodded. "Y-yes. I like books."

"Then I might have something for you-" Tillit mused as he stuck one arm into the depths of his bag.

Darda's eyes widened. "Shut that thing immediately!"

Tillit furrowed his brow. "Almost there-ah-ha!" He drew his hand out and revealed a book clutched in his fingers. Tillit held it out to Muffy. "I think you'll like this one."

"I-I really can't accept a gift," Muffy argued.

"Then you can borrow it," he suggested as he gave her a wink. "Just don't remember to return it."

A smile crept onto her lips as Muffy stepped forward and accepted the book. I scooted up to her side and read the title.

Adventures of A Daring Sus Through the Age of Maidens

I arched an eyebrow before I looked up at Tillit. "'Age of Maidens?'"

"You're not the only Maiden out there making a difference in the world," Tillit pointed out. He hitched up his pants and his smile widened. "Of course, the lead is a handsome sus who always finds himself in their troubles."

Darda snorted. "No doubt it is a comedy and a farce."

"Then this is your autobiography?" Muffy asked him.

Tillit nodded. "Yep. It's not finished, of course, but I'd like a second pair of eyes on it."

Muffy shook her head as she held it out to him. "I-I can't accept this. It's too important to you."

He snorted. "That's just my first draft. I've got a finer copy in my bag-" he patted the side of the satchel, "-so you're welcome to splash as much red ink as you want on that copy. It's your to keep."

Muffy clasped the book to herself and smiled at the sus. "Thank you."

"Mufid, we must attend to the others!" Darbat shouted from over the hill.

"Coming!" she called back. She bowed her head to us and hurried down the stone steps.

Darda turned to Tillit and glared at him. "Only you, Tillit, would believe that such a thing would be considered a 'gift.'"

Tillit grinned at her. "It's just one of the many ways I'm special, my dear Darda. Now what say we pitch in and help some of these flattened humans get on their feet?"

FOREST OF THE DRAGON

CHAPTER 18

No available horse nor strong back was spared as we hefted, carried, and leaned the fallen humans against us and our steeds. It was a long train of the ill with many of them so sick that they were unconscious, but still sneezing.

We reached Metsan after several long, arduous hours on the trail and found the citizens had turned out for our arrival. Dozens of fae waited for us outside the walls and helped us carry the ill humans to dozens of cots lined up in the lower halls of the trunks. The fae priests administered the antidote to everyone, even a few affected fae, and set the womenfolk to their nursing while they waited for the medicine to kick in.

I wiped my brow after setting another heavy, armored human onto a cot and looked around the long, circular hall. One cot against the trunk caught my eye, and I walked over to find Durion seated at Valo's bedside. Her breathing was still harsh, but her face wasn't so scrunched.

"How is she?" I asked him as I stopped at his side.

"She was one of those worst hit by the Metsä Nenä and will take a long while to recover, but she will have no lasting affects from the illness," he assured me.

I swept my eyes over the area. "Where's her dad?"

"He has returned to Reuna Kivet to fetch the remainder of his men."

I frowned. "So he left his daughter?"

"The human lord knows his obligation to his people must come before his concern for his daughter," Durion countered. He brushed a strand of hair from her cheek and pursed his lips as he studied her ashen face. "Can one such as I truly love a mortal woman such as she?"

My face softened as I glanced over my shoulder at where Xander stood with Tillit. Money changed hands before the intrepid sus gave a salute and hurried off. Xander returned to his helping lift the humans onto the cots. "I think-" I looked back to Durion and smiled at him, "-I think love cares more about what you do than who you are. When she wakes up I'm sure she's only going to see you sitting here, not some fae prince."

Durion looked up at me and a smile brightened his face. "Thank you for your kind words."

I swept my eyes over the sick room and sighed. "I wish I had more than that." Xander walked over to us with a grim expression. I winced. "Well? How bad is everyone?"

He glanced down at her and pursed his lips. "They inhaled a great deal of the dust of the forest, and they will need much care from the fae."

Durion pursed his lips. "My people are compassionate, but I do not know if the whole of Metsan contains enough food to feed so many mouths for even a short amount of time."

"I have instructed Tillit to have several of your traders go to the north and south to buy as many supplies as they need," Xander told him.

Durion turned back to Valo and sighed. "I thank you for your charity in this matter, but I fear we have a more grave concern. The god commanded that we ten return, but Valo is much too sick to partake of any games, much less those offered by a god."

Xander set a hand on his shoulder and smiled down at the young fae. "You will remain here with her. I am sure we eight will be able to match the wits and strength of one god."

The fae prince bowed his head. "But my people-"

"Will need a leader should the worst outcome occur," Xander insisted.

I frowned up at him. "Don't make it sound like we've already lost."

Xander sighed. "We must accept that that is a possibility. Only through the grace of one god did we defeat the last one."

My face fell. "Damn. I forgot about that."

Durion lifted his eyes to us and smiled. "I and all my people have faith in you and your friends. If anyone may defeat a god, it is through your power that such a miracle would happen."

We left the conversation on that uplifting note, but my heart was heavy as I went about caring for the sick and wounded. The day that had began so long ago ended and night fell. I wasn't even aware that I'd fallen asleep against a stack of blankets when a hand shook my shoulder.

My eyes fluttered open and I blinked wearily up into Darda's tense face. "What? Is it an attack by a giant ant?"

She shook her head. "No. The hour comes that we must return to the hill and face the god."

I ran a hand through my disheveled hair and sighed. "All right. Here we go."

The eight of us gathered at the entrance to the trunk palace. Thorontur swept his eyes over the group and frowned. "Where is my son?"

"He's going to stay with my daughter," Mies told him.

Thorontur's bushy eyebrows dropped down. "He was ordered by the god-"

"The god that's trying to evict you from your home," Mies reminded him.

"A god's command cannot be brushed aside to remain by the bedside of an ill person," Thorontur argued.

"Could we just get there and see if the god complains?" Tillit spoke up. "If we don't fit in with his games than dear Darda and Xander can go back for the two of them."

Mies nodded. "That would be a good idea."

Thorontur turned away, but didn't object, so we eight set off on horseback for Reuna Kivet. The dark forest was alive with the sounds of cawing night birds and the rustling of trees as predators stalked us in the deep shadows.

I stayed close beside Xander on the wide path, but looked to Thorontur who rode ahead of us with Mies at his side. "So you fae guys have all the creatures around here under control, right?"

He swept his eyes over the area as he shook his head. "No. There are creatures within this forest even we fae have not been able to tame."

"So those critters wouldn't happen to be night creatures, would they?"

A dozen dark shapes leapt from the forest and blocked the path ahead and behind us. They raised their furry heads and revealed themselves to be werewolves. Their red eyes fell on the fae king and their mouths snapped open to reveal long, sharp teeth.

My steed reared back as the others stopped theirs from dodging into the woods on either side of us. "I guess that answers my question."

Thorontur drew out the sword on his hip and raised it above his head. "Be gone, abominations! We go to do-"

FOREST OF THE DRAGON

"We don't care if you're going to go piss on an elm," one of the werewolves in the lead pack snapped, "-after all these years of being hunted by you fae we're finally going to let you have a taste of your 'game.'"

Thorontur glared at him. "We do not have time to discuss how you threaten our trade and our borders."

The werewolf hunched down on all fours and slowly approached the fae king. "Then make time."

The werewolves pressed in on our group as our horses tried to bolt. They snapped their jaws at the hoofs of our steeds. I wrapped my arms around my horse as it reared and whinnied. One of the werewolves lunged at me with its claws outstretched and its fangs aimed at my throat.

A rumble from the ground between the werewolf and me preceded the swift appearance of a column of grass and dirt. The column caught the werewolf in the gut and lifted it a towering fifty feet into the air. The column jerked to a stop, but the werewolf didn't. He flew off the top and landed somewhere deep in the forest.

The rumblings grew worse and more columns pushed from the ground around us. The other werewolves tucked tail and scuttled back into the woods. They disappeared from our view, but not because of the foliage.

The columns of dirt and grass continued to rise up around us, but not behind nor in front. Rather, they created a hallway with an open ceiling to the star-filled sky. Our horses pawed the ground for a few moments before they settled down.

Mies stroked the neck of his steed. "The horses consider us safe between these walls."

"I wish I could say the same. . ." I muttered.

"This must be the work of Lord Luoja," Thorontur mused.

I glanced to my right where a wall stood. On the wall was a single blooming pink flower like an orchid. "Or an expert gardener," I quipped.

"Regardless-" Xander spoke up as he turned his steed down the path, "-we must press on."

CHAPTER 19

We continued down the path unharassed and arrived just short of the appointed midnight hour. The wall of earthly columns stopped at the foot of the hill, so we left our horses tied to the trees at the bottom of the hill. We walked up the wide steps and into the circle of stones.

As the last of us entered the henge the area lit up with a greenish light that flitted around us. Everyone stiffened. I tracked one of the lights and saw they were small fireflies with their green-lit butts. They flitted among the stones like dancing ghosts. I hoped we wouldn't be mimicking them after these 'games.'

The earth trembled and a gaping hole opened in the same spot as before. The dirt elevator rose up and revealed Sala with a bright smile on his face. He rubbed his hands together as he swept his eyes over us. "My my, what a crowd-" he paused and frowned as he counted our number.

"Where are the other two? The fae prince and the lovely Valo?"

Mies stepped forward and glared at the god. "Valo's sick and the fae's at her side. You can play with us."

"If that suits you, My Lord," Thorontur added.

Sala shrugged. "It doesn't matter. There's too many people for the games I have in store, so I've decided to add a little more fun to the game."

Sala snapped his fingers. The ground rumbled and cracked beneath us. Vents opened wide and from them burst thick green vines. The vines wrapped around Darda, Xander, Mies, and Darbat, and lifted them off their feet.

Tillit leapt to catch Darda as she struggled in its grasp, but his porgy stature meant his feet left the ground only by a few inches. I and the others hand no better luck as our respective opposites were raised high into the air.

"Get this thing off me!" Mies snapped as he struggled in the grasp of the vines.

Sala shook his head. "I'm afraid not, My Lord. I don't see you as being good at games, but you'll make a great motivator for your friends."

I glared at the vines as I rolled my sleeves up. "All right, no more Normal Miriam."

"No!" Thorontur shouted at me. "Your water will only increase the vines!"

Sala laughed as a crack opened beneath him. A vine shot out, and on its green talk was a leaf of great width and length. The leaf lifted him off the ground so he hovered near our captured friends.

"Now isn't this fun?" he mused as his leaf weaved in and out of the vine-grasped others. "Doesn't this make it more *exciting* to have such high stakes?"

"Please let them go!" Muffy pleaded.

Sala dropped his leaf down close to her and shook his head. "I can't do that. If I let this many people play than it wouldn't be fair to me, would it?"

FOREST OF THE DRAGON

Thorontur shook his head. "But you are Lord-"

The young god whipped his head to the fae king and frowned. "I'm Sala. Sa-la. What you used to call me is boring."

While he blabbered on I noticed a change in my dragon lord. His body expanded outward and his wings sprang from his back. Darda, too, had wiggled a hand loose enough so that she tried to grab at a dagger hidden in her belt.

Sala noticed where my gaze lay and followed it. He frowned and floated his leaf up to them where he wagged his finger. "We can't have that."

The fireflies flew up from around us and surrounded our friends. They stuck their flickering rears in front of the trapped others and rocked from side-to-side. I followed their movement and found myself growing sleepy.

"Miriam!" Tillit yelled as he grabbed my shoulders and spun me around. My light head spun at his wrenching and made me clasp my forehead as the sus looked to Muffy and Thorontur. "Look away! Those are torkut bugs!"

Thorontur whipped his head away immediately, but Muffy was trapped in their mesmerizing sway. She took a step closer to where our friends hung above us, but Sala floated down and stopped in front of her. His smile was soft as he grasped her shoulders and turned her around. "Not you, Muffy. You get to play with me."

At the lost contact Muffy swayed from side-to-side. Sala released her so that she stumbled toward us. Tillit, careful to avoid the light from the bugs, grabbed her and helped her kneel on the ground.

Our trapped friends weren't so lucky. The bugs surrounded their heads so they had no way to look away, and the light from the torkut was so bright that even shutting their eyes they could still see the light in front of them. Their heads lolled back and their bodies went limp. Only their even breathing gave me comfort that they were okay.

Sala hovered in front of we four who remained and sat cross-legged on his leaf. "Now then, we have our players and our incentives."

My heart quickened as I remembered that Darda still held the chime beneath her dress. I glanced at her sleeping person, but couldn't see a bulge that indicated exactly where the chime box hung.

Sala swooped in front of my line of sight and chuckled. "Don't worry, I won't take the Theos Chime. This is going to be much more fun than merely stealing that stupid bell away from you." He held up a hand that displayed four fingers. "I have four tasks for you, one for each in your group, that you must solve to free not only your friends, but to lay claim to these woods. Fail, and I get to keep my title as Lord of the Forest *and* your friends."

"Who the hell do you think you are?" I snapped as I marched forward with sparks of water shooting from my fingertips.

Tillit grabbed my arm and held me back. "Not a good time to get mad," he whispered to me.

My hands clenched at my sides and glared at the god. "They're not pawns in this, so let them go!" I snapped at him.

"They're merely incentive for you to play the games I have for you," he argued as his eyes fell on Thorontur. "As a consolation to losing your friends I'll even let the fae king have his full powers, at least during these trials."

King Thorontur frowned at him. "What do you mean?"

Sala folded his arms across his chest and shrugged. "Just what I mean. After that last war between you and the humans I made sure to suppress the elemental powers of the fae so your kind couldn't make any more trouble, either."

Thorontur's mouth dropped open. "You robbed us of our strength? Of a power that defined us?"

Sala nodded. "Yep."

FOREST OF THE DRAGON

The fae king's mouth tightened as he narrowed his eyes at the god. "Then you are no god of ours."

Sala's eyebrows crashed down. "Don't make it personal. It was to save the forest."

"My people are very personal to me," Thorontur countered.

The god shrugged. "All right, take it personally, but don't let that interfere with the fun. Now-" he circled us on his leaf throne and opened his arms wide, "-on with the games!"

"What kind of games?" Tillit asked him.

"Let's call them 'growth games,'" Sala mused. His eyes flickered from one of us to the other as a smile danced across his lips. "I've studied you four since I first saw you, and I think I've devised the perfect game for each of you. However, it's up to you to figure out who best suits which game, and each person only gets one to play."

"Get on with it!" I snapped.

He grinned and held up one hand. "All right. Here we go."

Sala snapped his fingers. One of his vines slithered up to Thorontur and sprouted a small white flower. The flower burst open in his face, forcing him to inhale a deep mess of pollen. The ground opened up beneath us some ten feet in all directions. We dropped screaming into the darkness below us.

CHAPTER 20

Muffy and I screamed on the way down, but I think Tillit's squeal beat us on the highest pitch. The hole in which was dropped expanded and revealed to our frightened eyes a circular cavern as large as a stadium. The area was illuminated by countless clusters of torkut bugs that flitted out of our paths. At the bottom was a hard dirt floor that would've ended the game very soon if four round patches of grass hadn't risen up and met us halfway to our demise. We were lowered to the ground where the patches became one with the earth again.

I stood on my shaky legs and looked at the others as they did likewise. "Everybody okay?"

Muffy clutched the front of her shirt, but nodded. "I-I think so."

"Nothing a little pint at the Sus Tavi won't fix," Tillit replied.

FOREST OF THE DRAGON

Thorontur stood with his back to we three. He held his hands up in front of him with the palms facing upward. His wide eyes were glued to his palms

I took a step toward him and leaned to one side to catch his gaze. "You okay, King Thorontur?"

He lifted his head and pointed one of his palms toward the ground in front of him. The earth trembled a moment before a column of dirt, much like those created by Sala to chaperon us to the hill, rose up ten feet.

The fae king tilted his head back and gaped at the obelisk of dirt. "By all the gods. . ."

I stepped up to his side and looked from the column to his surprised face. "You couldn't do that before?"

He returned his attention to his hand and shook his head. "No. We fae are-or were-limited to the mere conjuring of piles of dirt for use in building bricks." A bitter chuckle parted his lips as he clenched his fist shut. "Now I find myself in possession of the ancient power of my ancestors that defeated so many threats, and yet I am powerless against the enemy we now face."

I jerked my thumb at the column. "You can't make a bigger one than that?"

He shook his head. "It is not the strength I now possess, but the source. The ancient tales of Lord Luoja-the creator-define him as the source of the power of we fae here in Virea Metsa. Therefore, we cannot go against him."

"Like fighting fire with fire," Tillit mused.

I furrowed my brow at the fae king. "But don't you have your own power? Like me?"

Thorontur stared ahead of us and pursed his lips. "Perhaps long ago, but legend tells of my forefathers making a pact with the creator that our power should strengthen his while he would guarantee us rule over the area."

"But only if you behaved," Sala spoke up. We looked up at where we'd fallen and watched him float down atop his vine-connected leaf. "You had to use your strength wisely, and after that little tiff between you and the humans I could see I'd given you a toy you were bound to abuse again."

"If you insist on locking away our powers then I demand an end to the agreement!" Thorontur insisted.

Sala smiled. "I might consider it, but first you have to play my games to even think about escaping from here."

"Where is 'here'?" I spoke up as I looked around at the rocky walls and earthen floor.

Sala stretched his arms out on either side of him. "This is my playground. Now-" he tapped his chin with one finger, "-what sort of field should we have?" His eyes flickered to the column created by Thorontur and he smiled. "Yes. I think that will work."

He snapped his fingers and tremors shook the earth and walls. Thick vines burst from the dirt and stretched upward to within twenty feet of the two-hundred foot tall ceiling. Leaves burst from the vines and tangled together to create a wall of green that surrounded us so that we stood in a circle. The foliage swallowed up Thorontur's column like it was a snack and the dirt tumbled out of sight beneath the wave of leaves.

Four paths revealed themselves, one each for the cardinal directions. We couldn't see too far down them because all the paths turned a ninety-degree corner and disappeared.

I looked around us and wrinkled my nose. "A hedge maze?"

Sala's plant had attached itself to the leaf-covered hedge walls so that he remained above us. "Yes. Isn't it beautiful?"

Tillit wrinkled his nose at all the greenery. "It's an overgrown bush."

Sala's eyebrows crashed down and his leaf drew a little further away from us. "Enough talk. Let's play a game." He swept one hand over the four paths. "Each of these paths leads to a different challenge. Face them by following the rules, and you'll get to see your friends in no time."

"How many of these 'games' do we have to win before our friends are let go?" I asked him.

He grinned. "*All* of them."

Thorontur frowned. "A better number would be three out of four."

"Maybe, but while this was your dragon lord's idea, these are my games, my rules," Sala countered. "Now-" he nodded at the paths, "-choose one and we can start."

I looked around at my friends. "I guess I can choose."

Tillit pulled up his pants and shook his head. "I'll go first, Miriam. My sus nose can sniff out the danger so we'll save the worst for last."

Sala chuckled. "Perhaps they're all equally as bad as the others."

The sus raised his piggish nose to the air and took in a deep whiff. He turned his head to the left and pointed down that path. "That way should be easy."

"How can you tell?" Muffy asked him.

Tillit tapped the side of his snout and winked at her. "This nose has seen enough trouble that it can sniff out mischief."

Thorontur scoffed. "We do not have time for your foolishness."

Tillit turned his nose up at the fae king. "It's no joke, and I can prove it to you with a walk down the path."

I took Muffy's hand and jerked my head in the direction of Tillit's path. "Come on. If there's anything I trust it's that nose."

Tillit led the way and Thorontur grudgingly followed behind us. Sala rose atop the hedge on his leaf and followed above our heads.

The maze was as winding as a snake sent through the tumble-dry setting of a dryer. The first corner was sharp, but the others zigged, zagged, curved, and, sometimes, abruptly stopped.

After a half hour of walking I glanced at our intrepid leader. "Tillit, I trust your nose, but not for walking distances. How much farther until this trouble?"

He took a whiff of the air. "I'd say we're just about-"

The earth trembled and the hedges around us gave way so that we stood in an open area some fifty feet circular. Dirt rose up from the ground and slipped over our heads, trapping us in a miniature version of the cavern. Muffy clutched onto me as the dirt blocked out all the light but for a small hole in the roof. Several clusters of torkut bugs floated through the hole and illuminated our small space, casting a blue light against the walls and on our faces.

A hole opened in the dirt and Sala floated down to us. He had a bright smile on his face as he clapped his hands. "A nice trick, sus, knowing where the game would be held by smelling where the change in the path was."

Tillit twitched his nose. "I'd rather be congratulated on winning one of your games."

I swept my eyes over the dirt-enclosed arena. "What kind of game is this? Dirt-slinging?"

The torkut bugs cast deep shadows on Sala's face as he hovered above us. "No. I don't like the dirt myself, but I had to guarantee that this area would have controlled darkness."

I frowned. "Why that?"

Sala snapped his fingers. Thorontur gasped. I whipped my head in the direction of the fae king. He took a step back and stared at a nearby wall. Against the wall, but not on it, stood his shadow. My heart skipped a beat when I recognized the dangerous form of a Sentinel.

Thorontur steadied himself and glared at his shadow. "Lakkaa varjo!" Nothing happened.

I glanced at Tillit, but jerked my head toward the fae. "What's that mean?"

"'Cease shadow.' It means he's telling him to come back," Tillit told me.

I looked between the fae and his still-standing shadow. "I don't think it's working."

Sala chuckled. "The sus didn't lead you astray with his nose. This is the easiest of my tasks. One of you, and only one of you, must defeat the Sentinel."

I slipped behind Muffy and grasped her shoulders. "I think this one's for you."

She whipped her head around to stare at me with wide eyes. "M-me?"

I nodded. "Yep. Xander told me these things are weak to wind, and you're the only wind user we've got."

Her mouth dropped open. "B-but I can't! I can't use wind!"

The Sentinel drew its long sword from its dark sheath and stalked toward us.

Tillit took a step back and glanced over to us. "Now would be a good time to practice!"

Thorontur stepped in front of us and held his arms out on either side of him. "As its master I believe this task is for me."

"But it isn't listening to you!" I pointed out.

"But I am at my full strength, and whatever insolence it wishes to perform is a mute point," he argued as he raised his arms up.

The earth shook, and huge columns of dirt and rocks rose up in front of us. Their tops slammed into the ceiling and their sides were so close to one another that they shaved stone off those beside them. In a few seconds there was a massive wall in front of us, one that blocked out the path completely.

He stepped up to the wall and smiled at his handiwork. "Not even a ray of light could penetrate such a wall."

The color drained from my face when I noticed a few of the torkut bugs crawl into the gaps between the rocks. "Tell that to *them*."

The bugs crawled inside and out of sight, but we could still see the glow of their butts. The lights cast shadows across the stone and dirt tomb, and through those cracks emerged Thorontur's shadow. The bugs increased the size of the Sentinel so that when it slipped out it was twice as big as before.

Sala chuckled. "It looks like your plan isn't working, fae king."

Thorontur's eyebrows crashed down. He raised his hands and summoned more rock columns, but the Sentinel was ready. The creature swung its weapon around itself, slicing through every pillar Thorontur could throw at it. With each swipe the Sentinel marched closer until the destruction of one of the columns flung bits of rock and dirt at the fae king.

Thorontur stumbled back and tripped over the floor. He fell backward onto his rear as the Sentinel stopped in front of him. The creature took a step forward and grasped its sword in both hands as it raised the weapon above the fallen fae king.

Thorontur flung up his hands on either side of him like an underhanded, ambidextrous pitcher. The stones on the floor around him, and many buried beneath the ground, shot up and built a wall between the fae king and the Sentinel. The Sentinel took a step back and drew his sword perpendicular to his side. He swung at the stone wall and his sword shattered the hard rocks. As fast as Thorontur could build it the shadow knocked them down.

In a few moments he would be skewered like a bit of meat on a kebab.

CHAPTER 21

I looked to Muffy. Her face was a picture of horror as she watched unblinking as the fae king's arms moved slower with every toss. "Come on, Muffy! You're the only one who can save him!"

She shook her head. "I-I-"

"-*can* do it," I insisted.

"I can't!"

I glanced at Tillit. He jerked his head toward Thorontur. Muffy remained frozen in place.

I set my hand on the lower part of her back and tensed my arm muscles. "You *can* do it, now go out there and-" I shoved her forward and, aided by my water magic, propelled her toward Thorontur, "-do it!"

Muffy's feet stumbled over the ground and she dropped unheroically onto Thorontur's lap so that she draped over him. The fae king glared at her as he tried to push her off him. "Foolish human! You are trying to get us both-ah!"

His Sentinel stood before them and raised his sword for a death stab. Muffy looked up with wide eyes as Thorontur did the same. She rolled over onto her back, shut her eyes, and flung up her arms to protect herself.

A blast of wind burst from her palms and hit the Sentinel. The creature's body rippled along with its sword so that when the weapon hit Muffy the shadow merely fell across her person. The Sentinel narrowed its eyes and leapt back ten feet.

I cupped my hands over my mouth. "Open your eyes, Muffy!"

Muffy creaked open one eye and swiveled it around the area. Her other eye popped open when she glimpsed her foe not standing triumphantly over her skewered body, but at a distance and glaring at her. She looked down at her hands and her mouth dropped open as she watched the two powerful tornadoes spin in her palms.

She lifted her hands close to her face and gawked at the wind. Her lips parted to whisper a few words. "By all the gods. . ."

"Do you mind removing yourself from my person?" Thorontur growled from beneath her.

"Oh! I'm so sorry!" Muffy scrambled to her feet and held her hand out to the rumpled fae king. "Are you all right?"

He ignored her hand and climbed to his feet. His eyes looked past her at his devious shadow before he tilted his gaze up to glare at Sala. "You would turn even my own shadow against me?"

Sala shrugged. "I think the irony is hilarious."

"I do not find it amusing."

Sala nodded in the direction in front of Thorontur. "Neither does he."

We all returned our attention to our dark foe. The Sentinel's form was once more solid as it raised its sword perpendicular to its side for a broad sweep. The creature dug its heels into the ground and set its sights on Muffy.

"Blow it away, Muffy!" I shouted.

"And the torkut bugs!" Tillit added as he swept his eyes over the glowing bugs that floated around us. "Without those there's no light for the shadow to form itself!"

Muffy cringed away from the shadow and took a step back. She bumped into a hard object and whipped her head up. Thorontur towered over her. His lips were pursed as he looked down into her frightened face, but he jerked his head toward his dark self. "Sweep that creature into oblivion and we shall win your match."

She bit her lower lip. "But-"

"You have the strength, now find the confidence," he told her.

Muffy swallowed hard as she looked back at the shadow that remained in place during their talk. The Sentinel leaned back in preparation for a charge and violent swing.

I furrowed my brow and leaned toward Tillit. "Is it just me, or did that homicidal shade wait for them to finish?"

Tillit's eyes flickered up to our host who floated close above the fae king and Muffy. "I'd say our game host is more interested in the journey than the destination."

"Meaning?"

"He's having too much fun to care about finishing us off."

Muffy swallowed the lump in her throat and stepped forward to face her foe. The wind in her hands flickered and nearly vanished. She reached up and opened her hand to clasp the front of her shirt, but she paused halfway. Muffy took a deep breath and lowered her hand back to her side. The mini tornadoes in her palms steadied and quickened, forcing Thorontur back as the winds whipped around her. Muffy stood unscathed in the eye of her own storm.

The Sentinel pushed off from the ground and rushed her. Muffy whipped one of her hands up as a reflex. A blast of air hit the Sentinel full on, pushing him back. The thing's feet dragged into the dirt and left long skid marks. Its form flickered, but reassembled itself. The torkut bugs that buzzed around its body were shoved against the far wall. Some of them were splattered against the dirt wall.

Muffy clapped her hands over her mouth. "Oh no! Those poor bugs!"

"Focus on the big one!" I shouted as I pointed a finger at the area in front of her.

Her gaze returned to the Sentinel. The creature sheathed his sword and drew a dagger from a concealed sheath hidden behind his waistband. I whipped my head to Thorontur and noticed an identical bulge.

"Were you going to tell us about that one?" I questioned him.

"At an opportune time," he assured me.

The Sentinel drew back the dagger for a throw. Muffy's eyes widened. The creature threw the shadow dagger at her head. She drew her hand away from her mouth and stretched her arm out in front of her. Her tornado swallowed the dagger and spun it around within its swirling body.

"Throw it back at him!" Thorontur instructed her.

Muffy drew back her arm before she threw her hand forward. The dagger flew out of the top of the vertical tornado and sailed past the Sentinel to embed itself deep into the dirt wall among another couple dozen smooshed bugs.

The Sentinel looked from the dagger to Muffy, and glared at her. She sheepishly smiled at it. The Sentinel turned and strode over to the wall. It grabbed the short hilt and gave a yank. The dagger remained in the wall. It narrowed its eyes and wrapped both hands around the handle before it started a tugging war with the wall. The wall was winning.

FOREST OF THE DRAGON

"Destroy the bugs while it is distracted," Thorontur told her.

Muffy pursed her lips, but raised her hands above her. The wind from the tornadoes sucked in all the bright bugs, creating two lanterns above her head. She flung her arms down in front of her, sending the tornadoes to the ground before her. The bugs went along for the ride until they were tossed out of the tops of the cyclones and into the wall, smashing them against the dirt.

The small dome we found ourselves in went dark except for the fading glow of the last of the bugs. The Sentinel yanked its dagger free and turned to us just as the last of the light vanished. Its bright eyes showed a sense of calm as it bowed its head to us and disappeared.

I couldn't see a damn thing, but I could Sala as he clapped his hands together. "Excellent! I didn't expect you to have such control so quickly. The human ability to achieve greatness under stress knows no bounds."

"The human capacity to see in complete darkness is not so great," I quipped.

"Right." He snapped his fingers. The earthen dome withdrew back into the ground and the hedges rose up to replace it, so that in a few seconds we stood once more in the maze. Sala floated over us on his leaf and smiled at Muffy. "That's game one to your side, Muffy. Good job."

She blushed and smiled. "Thank you."

I glanced at Tillit. "So where's the next challenge?"

He wrinkled his nose. "A long way off."

"Let me help you," Sala offered.

He snapped his fingers again, and a rectangular platform of the earth beneath us floated up, levitated by countless little torkut bugs. I yelped as the bugs flew down the maze at a speed that made me loose my balance. My feet flew out from under me and I would have fallen off the platform if Tillit hadn't caught me and pinned me to the ground.

He smiled at me as Thorontur and Muffy knelt in front of us. "Quite an adventure you've gotten me into," he teased.

I snorted. "How do *I* get off?"

CHAPTER 22

The platform flew us to the circular center of the maze where we had begun. The hedge wall closed behind us, leaving us with three paths to take.

Sala, who had kept up behind us, floated in front of us and gestured to the remaining paths. "Where will you go next?"

I looked to our resident trouble-hound. "Well?"

He lifted his nose and pointed at the path to our right. "That way."

"Then let me take you there," Sala offered.

I winced as the platform sped down that path. The wind whipped at my face and drew my hair behind me. Tillit choked on my flying threads and leaned a little back.

"I hope Xander's enjoying his nap," he commented as he waved my hair from his face.

I pursed my lips. "Me, too, because it's going to be a short one."

The previous half hour walk changed to a two-minute ride. The platform stopped abruptly and sank into the ground. We climbed to our feet and found ourselves in a long path that stretched to the wall of the game coliseum. The path shut around us again and we were soon encased in another dirt-encrusted dome.

"To avoid the debacle of last time-" Sala floated in front of Thorontur and swept his arm over the room, "-fae king, I present to you your game."

In the center was a perfectly round stone that was as tall as me. At the opposite end was a hoop made of roots. On either side of us in the floor were wide holes that followed the rounded contour of the room like slots. The holes were large enough to fit even Tillit's girth with ease.

"Your objective is for you to throw the rock into the bottomless basket without the stone dropping into the chasm more than twice. After the third drop, you *all* drop into the chasm."

Thorontur stepped forward with a grin. "I will gladly do this-"

"Wait a moment. I'm not done," Sala told him. His eyes fell on Muffy as she stood beside me. "You have to combine Mufid's wind magic with your own earth magic to get the stone into the hoop."

The fae king started back and his eyes widened. "Use an opposing magic? That is impossible to control!"

"Not impossible, just really hard," Sala argued as his leaf floated close beside the hoop. "You can start any time you're ready."

"Wait a minute!" I spoke up as I stalked to the head of our group. "You told us that each of us was only going to get one game!"

Sala grinned. "Did I? I guess I misspoke. What I meant to say was that each of you would get only one game, *or* you might help out one of your friends in theirs."

FOREST OF THE DRAGON

Thorontur frowned. "I have no need of the human's help. My powers are quite capable of handling this task."

"It's his house, so it's his rules," Tillit reminded him.

"If you value your trade in my city than you will be quiet," Thorontur threatened him.

The sus snorted. "I value my life more, and that's not going to be around long if you don't follow the rules, or at the very worst bend them a little."

"There is no need for bending. I have my powers returned to me, and those will simplify this task to mere child's play."

Thorontur raised up one hand and from the ground beneath the stone rose thick green vines. They wrapped around the boulder and lifted the heavy rock off the ground like it was a balloon. He flicked his wrist in the same motion as a basketball player making a shot. The vines mimicked his movement and flicked the stone into the air.

Dirt vines greater than his drew out from the walls and swatted the rock down like it was a basketball and they the defense. The stone slammed into the ground and rolled into the chasm.

Sala chuckled. "See what happens when you don't both play? You lose." A gray speck appeared in the ground and grew larger until a full boulder stood in the same spot the first one had started. "Now it's time to try again, but this time do it right."

Thorontur turned his head and his narrowed eyes fell on Muffy. "Come up here."

I set my hands on Muffy's shoulders and frowned at him. "She has a name."

His eyes never left her. "That is inconsequential compared to her abilities as a wind caster. Do you have the skill to assist me?"

Tillit snorted. "She just saved your hide."

"Well? Do you?"

Muffy bit her lower lip, but stepped forward. "I. . .I can try."

"There is more than 'trying' needed for this task," he countered as he gestured to the rock. "We must combine our powers into a storm of wind and vines that will ensure the boulder is safely deposited through the circle."

She nodded. "I understand."

Thorontur turned his full attention on the rock and held out his hands. "Good, then I will wrap my vines around the stone and you will toss the boulder through the hoop."

Thorontur wrapped his vines around the stone. Muffy took a deep breath and raised her hands so her palms were pointed upward. Small tornadoes appeared on her palms. She pursed her lips and tossed her tornadoes underhand at the stone like a child throwing a ball for the first time.

The tornadoes combined and hit the side of the stone. The force pushed the rock across the floor and into the chasm.

Sala let out a great laugh as another boulder appeared from the ground. "That's two! One more and I win!"

Thorontur spun around to face Muffy with all the ire of a cheated king. "You fool! How could you make such an incompetent move?"

Muffy shrank back from his anger. "I-I'm sorry. I-I-"

"Failed on this account," he interrupted her as he sneered down at the small human. "It appears your victory in the prior game was merely a fluke."

"Knock it off, Thorontur!" I snapped. "She's only trying to help!"

"She would do better to stand back and use as little power as possible so that I might finish this task," he suggested.

FOREST OF THE DRAGON

I glanced at Muffy. "Come on, Muffy, don't let him run you over like that. You've already shown your stuff, so show it again."

Muffy clutched the front of her chest, took a deep breath, and straightened to her full short height. "King Thorontur-" his eyes flickered to her, "-for the sake of both our people we must help one another."

Thorontur started back and stared at her with unblinking eyes. His face softened and he looked ahead at the boulder. A few whispered words passed his lips. "Have I. . .perhaps-" he closed his eyes and shook his head. "What a fool. What a plaything of the gods I have been."

Sala chuckled. "But you've been such an interesting player."

Thorontur raised his eyes to the god and glared at him. "I have no doubt I have been so, but no more." He whipped his head to Muffy and held out his hand to her. "For my people-for *both* of our people-we must succeed."

Muffy smiled and took his hand before she gave a nod. "For both our people."

Sala rolled his eyes. "This is all very touching, but it won't get that boulder any closer to the hoop."

Tillit snorted. "Then you don't know Miriam's friends."

Muffy looked from the stone to Thorontur's tense face as he, too, studied the boulder. "What do you want me to do?"

He nodded at the bottom of the stone. "Try to lift the boulder off the floor, and I will guide the stone to its place."

She nodded. "I'll more than try, I'll succeed." The corners of Thorontur's mouth twitched up, but he merely returned her nod with one of his own.

Muffy stepped forward and held out her upturned palms. The tornadoes reappeared, but instead of throwing them she pressed her hands together, combining the cyclones into a swirling wind tunnel. She knelt on one knee and gently set the cyclone on the ground. The whirling wind was still for a moment before it made a zig-zag line for the boulder. The tornado slipped under the stone and lifted the heavy boulder.

Thorontur summoned his vines and they once more wrapped around the stone. He clenched his teeth as he focused on pulling the boulder across the floor between the chasms and into the hoop.

Sala clicked his tongue as he shook his head. "Not enough on Muffy's part."

The next moment his vines shot out of the wall and latched onto the boulder. They tipped the stone off Muffy's tornado and it fell into the left-side chasm. Thorontur clenched his teeth and wrenched his arms toward himself. His vines suspended the ball a mere foot from the hole. Sala's vines wrapped around his and held him in place.

"Remember the rules," Sala scolded him. "The ball can't be moved without both of you moving it."

Muffy's hands shook as she tried to move her tornado toward the ball. The spinning air slipped under the net and rattled the dry wood that made up the hoop. She froze as her eyes widened, and she whipped her head to Thorontur. "Please keep the ball as still as possible!"

"Hurry your wind to me!" he snapped.

Muffy furrowed her brow as she tried to squeeze her hands together. The body of the tornado mimicked her movements and shrank, trapping the hoop within itself. The violent winds tore the hoop from the wall and sent it spinning within the tornado.

Thorontur whipped his head to her tense face and frowned. "What are you-" his eyes widened as she tilted the tornado and set the hoop hovering in the middle of the storm. "By all the gods!"

FOREST OF THE DRAGON

Tillit let loose a laugh as he slapped his leg. "Now that's human ingenuity! If you can't control the ball then control the net!"

Muffy slipped the hoop in the narrow space between the chasm and the boulder. Thorontur released the boulder and the huge stone sailed through the hoop before it disappeared into the chasm. Muffy's wind died out and the hoop followed the stone. The earth shook as it folded over the chasm, dropping Muffy to the ground as the dirt walls around us sank back into the rising hedges.

Sala clapped his hands. "An excellent display of teamwork! And such an ingenious way of getting it through the hoop! That's the fun I've been waiting for!"

Thorontur stooped in front of Muffy and held his hand out to her. "You performed well. For a human, that is."

Muffy smiled and accepted his hand so that he pulled her to her feet. "Thank you, King Thorontur, but you deserve as much credit as I."

The fae king drew back his hand and half-turned away from her so he faced the god. "Yes, well, to the victors go the spoils. We have won, Sala, and within your rules."

Sala shrugged. "So you have, but I still have a few more fun games up my sleeve. Now-" he snapped his fingers and the rectangular platform once more lifted us off the ground, "-let's see if you can win again."

CHAPTER 23

We were zipped back to the central circle where only two paths were left to us. Tillit sniffed the air and pointed at the one opposite us. "There."

Sala grinned. "An excellent choice, Mr. Tillit. Now let's see what you chose."

The platform bolted into the path and flew us to the far wall of the cavern. We were set onto the floor and once more encased in a dirt dome.

At the opposite end, some twenty feet from where we stood, rose three trunk-like pedestals from the floor. Atop each was a metal box, each nearly identical to the others. On the clasp of each one was a small image. One image was that of a chest, the other a large diamond, and the third was a crown.

Tillit strode to the front of our group and stretched out his arm across our paths. "I think this one's mine."

I frowned at him. "How can you tell?"

FOREST OF THE DRAGON

He lifted his piggish nose to the air and sniffed. "Because if I'm not mistaken those boxes are full of some nice valuables."

"Correct on both counts," a voice spoke up. We raised our gazes to the ceiling and watched Sala, seated cross-legged on a large leaf, float down to twenty feet above us. A Cheshire grin graced his lips as his eyes fell on our sus friend. "This is your challenge, Mr. Tillit, and a strange one for a sus. For one of your kind, and you can believe I've seen many of your kind venture through my forest-"

"Not for long," I quipped.

He chuckled at me. "Not if he can't get this right." He returned his attention to Tillit. "You place quite an emphasis on friendship over profit. Now we're going to put that policy to the test. These boxes-" he gestured to the three on the pedestals, "-contain the items you listed, but which one best defines your friendship?"

Tillit wrinkled his nose. "If those are the choices than I'm choosing friendship. It keeps longer than any of them."

Sala shook his head. "That's no way to play a game. You have to choose one, but I'll give you a hint in the form of a riddle: within me I hold life and death, without me is loneliness. Kings prize me, women size me." The god leaned back and folded his arms over his chest. "Well? Go get it."

Tillit snorted. "That's an easy one." He walked up to the box with the crown on the front and snatched the box from the pedestal. The ground shook and the pedestals sank into the ground. Tillit turned to Sala and held up the box. "I think that makes you the loser again."

Sala sneered at him. "That was a lucky guess."

Tillit shook his head. "You forgot, Mr. God, that this sus can read, and I've read more than one book mocking the 'mushroom crowns' atop the heads of kings."

Sala gestured to our resident royal. "My riddle might have fooled you if he wouldn't wear his crown so much."

Thorontur reached up and grasped his crown as he frowned. "My crown is perfectly suited to my head."

Sala snorted. "It looks like a melon on top of a grape."

The fae king narrowed his eyes and dropped his hand to near his face where his energy illuminated his palm. "You may be more powerful than I, my former lord, but-"

"-but I'm getting bored of this talking," Sala interrupted as he covered a fake yawn with his mouth. He paused mid-fake and a sly smile slipped onto his lips. The god dropped his hand and rose a little higher above us. "That was too easy for you, Mr. Tillit, so I'm going to add a little bit more fun to your game."

"We played your game," I snapped as I moved to stand between Tillit and the rest of my group. I looked up at Sala and pointed at the walls around us. "Just open those up so we can beat your ass one more time."

The god chuckled as his leaf floated higher. "You might regret your impatience, child of contradictions, for I have something special in store for you." A round hole opened in the wall again and he disappeared through it.

I balled my hands into fists at my side and glared at where he'd gone. "Asshole. . ."

"What did he mean by 'child of contradictions?'" Muffy spoke up.

Thorontur pursed his lips as he studied me. "There is no place in the world of the fae for one who is only half our kind, nor is there a place in our world for a human of the other one."

I shook myself and took a deep breath. "It's fine. Let's just beat him one more time and get everyone back."

There was the usual shaking, but the walls around us didn't open. Rather, the wall to our right parted and revealed another long hall.

Tillit wrinkled his piggish nose. "Looks like he was serious about me playing again. Well-" he pulled up his pants

FOREST OF THE DRAGON

and straightened, "-let's see if ol' Tillit can figure this one out in record time." Tillit and Thorontur strode forward into the tunnel.

I jumped when a hand touched my shoulder and whipped my head around to find Muffy behind me. Her soft eyes searched mine. "Are you sure you're all right?"

My shoulders drooped and I pursed my lips. "No, but I'll be fine."

She dropped her eyes to the ground and bit her lower lip. "I-um, when I'm feeling down, I-well, I talk to my parents."

I furrowed my brow. "You're not an orphan?"

She shook her head. "No. I mean, my parents are dead, but-" she drew her hand into her shirt and pulled out a small gold chain. Her hand was clasped around a larger object, and she opened her fingers to reveal a small locket. The parts were open and before me lay two small, dried flowers. "These were their favorite flowers. They gave them to me so I'd always remember them."

I smiled at her, but shut her hand and shook my head. "I can't take this. It's too important to you. Besides, I'll be fine. It's just words, right?"

I started back as Muffy opened my other hand and pushed the locket into my palm. "You need to-that is-" she raised her eyes and met my gaze with a steady one, "-you sometimes forget that you're not alone. No matter what anyone thinks of you, you've got friends around you that don't care, and don't want you to care about it." She paused and shrank back. "That is, that's what I think."

I smiled and wrapped her in a nice, tight hug before I parted us. "Thanks for the pep talk. I'll use this-" I held up her locket, "-as my lucky charm for now, but I'll give this back to you when we're out of here, okay?"

She looked up at me and smiled. "Okay."

"You two coming?" Tillit shouted at us from the opening.

"Keep your snout on!" I scolded him as I set a hand on Muffy's shoulder. I looked down and grinned. "Let's go beat this god."

She nodded, and together we joined Tillit and Thorontur. The long hall ran for a hundred yards before we found ourselves in another circular area. At the three other points were marble statues of women in various states of undress. One wore a thin cotton dress, another was hidden behind her long hair that trailed down the front of her body like a snake, and the third was covered by a thick fur bikini ensemble that left little to the imagination.

Sala floated behind the statues with a Cheshire grin on his lips. "All right, Mr. Tillit, let's see if you can solve this mystery."

Tillit stepped to the front of our group and hitched up his trousers. "I'm ready."

Sala cleared his throat. 'I slumber long within the ground, atop the head I may be crowned. Within the dirt I can be found, but not when shoes are to be bound. Which maiden am I?'"

Tillit snorted as he strode over to the woman with the fur outfit. "Your riddles are as old as you are." He turned to face the god and jerked his thumb behind him. "It's this one."

Sala frowned. "That was another lucky guess."

Tillit folded his arms across his ample chest and shook his head. "Nope. A bear slumbers, its fur is made into caps, bare feet are in the dirt, but not when someone's wearing shoes."

I studied the statues and wrinkled my nose. "So that's why the snake hair wouldn't work because it doesn't have feet."

Tillit nodded. "Exactly, and the cotton won't work because cotton shoes aren't bound, but sewed."

Muffy clapped her hands, and Thorontur and I followed her example. I put a few fingers into my mouth and whistled. Tillit turned to us and crossed his arm over his chest before he gave us a deep bow.

"Let's try another one." We all whipped our heads to Sala who sat sullen on his leaf. He wore a frown that marred his good looks as he rubbed his chin in one hand. "That one was too easy, too. Maybe I should play another game with you."

"Okay, that's enough," I snapped as I strode up to stand before his leafy highness. "We agreed that you could make the games, but not for the rest of our lives. We want our friends back some time this century."

The god shrugged. "What's that to me?"

Muffy frowned. "Sala, that is very rude."

"Rude, but true," he argued as he floated away from me. "And what can you do to stop me?"

I glared at him, and in doing so noticed his cheek. There was a slight reddish mark where the mud had slapped him earlier in the day. A sly smile slipped onto my lips as I folded my arms across my chest.

"I can't do anything to stop you," I told him.

He grinned. "Then it's pointless to argue with me, isn't it?"

I shook my head. "I said *I* can't do anything to stop you, but *we*-" I gestured to my friends, "-can."

Sala's face fell as he frowned. "What can so few of you do to a god?"

I slipped between Thorontur and Muffy. "We can put some nice mud makeup on your face."

Thorontur furrowed his brow as he studied me. "What do you mean?"

I slipped my arms over their shoulders and nodded at Sala's cheek. "You see that mark? It was made by the mud that the wind, vines, and water conjured up earlier."

Sala scoffed. "You believe that a combination of your powers can actually do me damage?"

I held out my hand in front of me and a pool of water formed in my upturned palm. "I don't know, but-" I looked from Muffy to Thorontur, "-I'm willing to try. How about you guys?"

Muffy smiled and stretched her hand out near mine before a tornado appeared on her palm. "I'm with you, Miriam."

Thorontur held out his hand and vines grew from the ground into his palm. "I will stay by your side, Neito Vedesta."

Their elements fused into my hand and created a greenish, wet mini tornado that tickled my palm. I held up the weapon to Sala and grinned at him. "You want some of this, or do we finish these 'games?'"

Sala's eyes widened as he floated further away from us to the edge of the dirt dome. "You can't do this! It's against the rules!"

"Your rules, maybe, but right now we're not playing any of your games right now," I countered.

Sala narrowed his eyes at me. "Very well." He snapped his fingers.

The floor beneath our feet opened and we dropped into a deep, dark hole.

CHAPTER 24

The drop was long and the landing wet as we found ourselves falling to the bottom of a deep pool of water. The darkness confused my senses and for a moment I almost swam downward, but one of my dragons erupted from my hand and drew me in the right direction. I broke through the surface and breathed in a deep breath of sweet, precious air.

We were in a deep well with smooth sides made of wet stone. The floor from which we fell was fifty feet above us, but with the slick walls it may as well have been a thousand. My feet couldn't touch the bottom and the cracks between the stones were so small that a mouse couldn't cling to them.

My three companions resurfaced around me, but with varying results. Tillit floated on the water, but Muffy and Thorontur made a splashy show of reappearing. They kicked their arms and legs without synchronization so that they wasted a lot of energy.

Sala's voice resounded through the rocky walls of the deep well, but we couldn't see him. "You wanted your last test, child of contradictions, so here it is: you have to get out of this well."

I swam to the side and pressed my hand against the smooth wall. The surface was like glass. I swam to near the center of the pool and tilted my head backward to look up at the ceiling. At the top of the conical room was a circular opening. The weak light from the small hole was amplified by the shiny walls and illuminated the deep well.

I stretched up one of my arms and a dragon slid out. My little pet stretched upward and through the opening. I smiled and looked at my friends. "I think this one's going to be an easy one again, guys."

Sala's chuckle echoed against the wall. "On the contrary, I've made some special rules for this one. First-" I heard his fingers snap together.

The calm surface of the water became marred by violent waves. A wave splashed over me and shoved me toward the wall, but didn't push me under. The water collided with the walls, worsening the height and strength of the waves. One of them dunked me, and when I broke the surface again I heard a cry from Muffy.

A wave of water washed over her as her arms flailed above her head. "Miriam!" she shrieked as her head sank only to reappear. "I can't swim!"

Thorontur choked on some water. "Nor can I!"

"I'm coming!" I yelled back as I summoned four dragons.

A hole opened in one of the walls above our heads and Sala floated out, perched on his leaf. He shook his head as he raised his hand. "None of that." He snapped his fingers.

Four thick roots drew themselves from the walls and wrapped around my dragons. Their succulent bodies absorbed my dragons, leaving not even a seahorse-sized body to save my friends.

Sala lowered himself close to us and smiled. "That leads me to my other rule. I'll only allow you enough energy to save yourself and two of your friends. So-" he swept his arm over my struggling friends, "-which species will you choose to save? The sus, the fae, or perhaps the human? Kith, kin, or kind? I await your answer with interest."

I pursed my lips and whipped my head back to my friends. Tillit bobbed up and down, but the waves pushed him around like a rubber ducky on the rough ocean. Thorontur and Muffy struggled to keep their heads above water. I summoned two of my dragons and slipped them beneath Muffy and the fae king. The raised them above the waves and the pair coughed out an unhealthy quantity of liquid.

Tillit's voice made me glance at him. "You should go."

I frowned at him. "Go where?"

He nodded at the opening far above us. "Go there, back to Xander. I'll-" a wave splashed over him and dunked him before he reappeared, "-I'll be fine." He paused and snorted. "Pity. I thought my book would last a little longer than this, but it looks like I'm the odd sus out."

My mind buzzed with thoughts, but none of them were a plan to get out of this with a happy ending. My gaze wandered over my friends. Their wide eyes, their bobbing heads, their hands as they clutched onto my dragons. I couldn't choose among them.

I caught sight of Muffy's locket. The precious trinket had been freed by the waves from my pocket and now floated in front of me. I snatched the locket and looked at the smooth surface.

My mother saved me.

I closed my eyes and clenched my hand around the locket. Her choice wouldn't be wasted.

I turned to Tillit and smiled at him. "Hey, Tillit, could you do me a favor?"

He fended off a wave and arched an eyebrow at me. "I don't think now's the time-"

"Could you remind Xander that I love him?"

Tillit's eyes widened. "What-"

"Not that I think he'll forget, but just as a last favor, okay?" I pleaded.

He shook his head. "Miriam, no. Don't do this. There's got to be another way."

I swam away from him and gave a small wave. "Be seeing you."

"Miriam!" Tillit yelled as he swam toward me.

My third and final dragon rose up beneath Tillit and captured him in its jaws. Tillit stretched out his hand to grab me, but he missed by a mile as the dragon shot him up toward the hole.

I turned to Muffy and Thorontur. The fae king pursed his lips. "I would rather be left behind."

I grinned. "You don't have a choice." I looked to Muffy and tossed her the locket. "Thanks for the lucky charm. It worked."

She clutched the locket to herself and shook her head as tears sprang to her eyes. "I-I can't let you do this. Please let me stay behind."

I shook my head. "Nope. You two behave now. No more fighting."

My dragons shot up, taking my last two friends with them. I tilted my head back and watched them slip out of the opening and onto dry land. I'd done it. I'd saved them *and* won.

A huge wave fell upon me and shoved me deep into the water. I tried to swim to the surface, but wave after wave of water knocked into me, wrenching the air from my lungs. My body pleaded for air, and I couldn't stop myself from

FOREST OF THE DRAGON

opening my mouth. Water rushed into my lungs. My mind started to drift off as I sank deeper into the bottomless pool.

Something soft and solid floated under me. I could barely comprehend the movement as I was lifted through the water to the surface. I broke into the life-giving air and coughed out what felt like a bucketful of water. My eyes flickered down to my savior. It was a large, leafy vine. The plant lifted me up the well and deposited me face-down on the dirt floor where I spat out more water.

My friends crowded around me with Tillit rolled me onto my back, but kept me upright so the water escaped my mouth. "That saves both of us," he teased as he pressed me against his side. I blinked wearily up at him and he smiled. "Xander would have killed me if I told him you didn't make it."

Thorontur checked my eyes and set his hand over my heart. "Weak, but no damage."

Muffy grasped one of my hands in hers and stopped the flow of tears that stained her cheeks. "Please don't do anything like that again."

I managed a weak laugh that spit out some water. "I'm not planning on it." Sala floated in my field of vision, and I smiled up at him. "Saved by a deus ex machina."

His expression was tense as he studied me with a careful gaze. "I think I've had enough games."

He snapped his fingers. The dirt dome collapsed, but the hedge didn't reappear. The ground beneath us was levitated by his vines, and together with our host we flew up toward the curved ceiling. The bugs and ceiling parted, revealing a long tunnel above our heads. We flew up through the hole and found ourselves back where we started in the ring of stones atop Reuna Kivet.

Our captured friends remained as we'd left them, asleep in the grasps of the vines. The platform beneath us became a part of the ground and sealed the hole to the subterranean cavern. Tillit helped me to my feet as Sala floated behind our friends.

His vines lowered our companions to the ground and unwrapped themselves from their bodies. Muffy and Thorontur hurried over to their counterparts, Darbat and Mies, while Tillit helped me over to Darda and Xander. Their eyes fluttered open as we reached them.

Xander's eyes widened and he shot up. He whipped his head around and his gaze fell on my bedraggled appearance. "Miriam!" Tillit handed me over to Xander where I embraced him in a tight hug. He drew us apart and looked me over. "What has happened to you?"

I choked out some water before I looked up at him. "Let's just say that next time we should just ring the damn bell."

He chuckled as he gave a nod. "Agreed."

CHAPTER 25

"Are you injured?" Darda asked me as Tillit and she came up to us.

I shook my head. "Nope. I had some good friends to keep me out of some of the trouble Sala put us through."

I swept my eyes over the rest of our group. Muffy helped Darbat to his feet as he looked down at her. "I hope you weren't too much of a burden for them."

"On the contrary-" Thorontur spoke up as he walked over to the pair with the drowsy Mies leaning against his side. "Your apprentice here showed quite a good amount of tenacity, courage, and wind skill. That is-" a ghost of a smile curled the corners of his lips up as his eyes flickered to Muffy, "-for a human."

Muffy returned the smile and bowed her head to him. "Thank you, King Thorontur."

Mies arched an eyebrow as he studied the fae king. "That almost sounded like a compliment."

Thorontur cleared his throat. "Yes, well, perhaps not all humans are contemptible. There may even be enough consideration on my part so that you might reside in your ancient city."

Mies smiled. "And the surrounding territory?"

"We shall discuss that later."

Darbat stood straight as he looked down at his apprentice with a hint of a smile on his lips. "Well, if that's the case then you'll have to show me some of these new 'skills' at the camp."

Tears sprang to Muffy's eyes as she wrapped her arms around him. "I'm so glad to see you again. I didn't think I ever would."

The father's eyes widened for a moment before his face softened. He returned the gesture and looked down with a smile at the young woman. "I'm glad to see you safe, as well."

"Touching, but you humans and fae really need to start packing," Sala spoke up as he hovered down to near our level atop his leafy perch.

I whipped my head to him and frowned. "Why? We won."

He shook his head. "Technically, I won."

My eyebrows crashed down as I marched over to him. "Like hell you did! I got my friends out by only using three dragons! That was the rule!"

"But *I* saved *you*-" he pointed out, "-so that means you owe me a win, and that makes me the winner of everything."

Muffy broke from her hug and frowned at Sala. "That isn't fair, Sala, and you know it!"

"Your childish rules are unbecoming of a god," Thorontur added.

Sala chuckled. "As a god I don't really care."

My gaze ghosted over Darbat and Muffy, clasped as they were. An idea struck me.

FOREST OF THE DRAGON

I folded my arms across my chest and shrugged. "All right, you win."

Darda stood a few feet away and looked aghast at me. "Miriam! We cannot let him cheat us in this fashion!"

I shook my head. "He made the rules, so he gets to decide who wins. That means he gets the whole forest all to his lonesome, but I don't think he's going to like it."

Sala arched an eyebrow. "Why wouldn't I like my own forest back?"

"I didn't say that," I argued.

"Then what are you implying?" he snapped.

I shrugged. "Just that it'll be all yours. *Just* yours. You can have your pets-" I waved my hand at the lentaja, "-fly everywhere to keep everyone out, and then you can play with yourself for the rest of your really, really, *really* long life."

Sala's face fell and his eyes widened. "I'll be. . .alone. . ."

"*Or* you could let us ring that bell and you can go home and play with all your old friends for as long as you want," I suggested.

A sly smile slipped onto his lips as he swept his eyes over our group. "Or I could keep you here and have you play with me again."

Well, there went *that* plan. My eyes flickered to Darda. One of her hands was easing toward the chime box. I stepped forward closer to Sala and smiled up at him. "That sounds like a-Darda!"

Darda lifted her skirt and drew out the chime box. Sala cried out in fury like an injured animal and snapped his fingers on both hands. The earth rumbled and vines sprouted from the ground beneath her. I drew out dozens of my smallest dragons and wrapped them around the vines, binding them together around Darda as she clutched the box to her chest.

Sala laughed. "Have you forgotten what water does to my plants?"

I shook my head. "Nope." I pushed more water into my dragons, and the vines absorbed the water until they were fat and swollen. Spouts of water burst from their veins and they dropped to the ground in a flailing mess as their bodies split apart. I grinned up at Sala. "How's that much water for you?"

He clenched his teeth and snapped his fingers again. More vines came up. I prepared myself for another attack, but before I could fire off my dragons two blades made of wind passed by me. They cut the vines at the base. I whipped my head around and found Darbat standing close behind me with his hands raised

He smiled at me. "I will show you the full power of a desert caster." He flung his hands in front of him and released four sharp blades of wind. They cut more vines and circled back for another pass.

Muffy created her own tornadoes and used them to shove the vines away from Darda. "Escape now!"

Darda rushed out of the vine trap, but more sprouted. A sword came down on those, and I looked to find it was Mies who held the blade. He looked up at Sala and grinned. "I've waited too long for this forest for a spoiled god to ruin everything now."

A vine whipped out and wrapped around the blade of his sword. Mies clenched his teeth and pulled, but the vine held tight. Another vine came up on his side and wrapped around the plant that held him down. The vines tangled together and drew off his weapon as they fought until both lay in pieces.

Mies looked behind him at Thorontur who had his hands raised and a small army of his own vines behind him. "Thanks."

Thorontur bowed his head. "I would do no less for an ally."

FOREST OF THE DRAGON

Sala floated high above us and his unearthly light burst out of him in a reddish color. "Stop it! All of you just stop it!"

The top of Reuna Kivet became a battlefield once more, but between two very different armies from times past. Vines thick and small burst from the ground around the stones while a few taimet appeared at the base of the hill. Xander leapt from the hill and flew down to meet the tree creatures, and as he did his body transformed into his full, monstrous dragon form. He landed atop one and broke it to pieces. The others rushed him, but his tail and teeth kept them at bay.

Darda drew out her dagger with one hand and hacked away at the vines as wind, vine, and blade, along with enough water to fill the Great Lakes, pounded them back.

The lentaja screeched and rushed toward us. Tillit dropped his bag and rummaged inside for a few moments before he drew out his long cannon. He shouldered the hefty weapon and aimed it at the flying creatures. A deafening blast announced the arrival of more fun as he shot a wad of the vampiri de hârtie at the plant butterflies. Bug met bat in an epic showdown that resulted in all the creatures crashing to the forest floor.

Sala wasn't losing, but he wasn't winning against us, either. He narrowed his eyes on me as I flung aside more of his bloated vines. They burst asunder on the ground, sending out green blood-like ooze. I looked up and dodged a blow from a vine that grew from his own palm.

He floated down to my level and glared at me. "Why don't you want to play with me? What could be more fun than living a life of games?"

"That's not the kind of life I want, or my friends," I snapped back.

He raised his hand that held the vine above his head and pursed his lips. "All right. Let's end this."

I nodded at the area behind him. "I already have just by talking to you."

Sala gasped as a mess of vines wrapped around *him*. They pulled down his arm and pinned both of them to his sides. A tornado wrapped around him while a wind blade cut the leaf from its stalk so that both god and leaf tumbled to the ground. He rolled onto the dirt where my dragons slithered around his body so he was trapped in a swirling mess of mud. Sala twisted onto his side and looked up into the unsmiling faces of my friends as we crowded around him. Many of his own creations lay dead or dying, and those that were still in a fighting mood hesitated at his capture.

I stepped up to him and Darda moved to my side where she handed me the box. Sala's eyes widened as I drew the bell out, but a bitter smile slipped onto his lips. "I see. It looks like I really did lose against you, child of contradictions."

I shook my head as my companions came to surround him and me. "Nope. You lost against Miriam the Maiden and her trusty friends."

He chuckled. "I see. A power that could change the world more than any god."

I raised the bell and rang it. The chime echoed over the stones and grass. The vines that remained dropped to the ground and were absorbed. Sala's form began to disappear as he sighed.

His last few words drifted across the air as he disappeared completely. "Maybe Phrixus will play with me again. . ."

Thorontur's vines dropped to the empty ground. I lowered the chime and sighed. It was over.

I swore I'd never play another game again.

CHAPTER 26

A rumbling made me jump and spin around. Xander walked up the hill in his full dragon form. Below him were the remains of the taimet. On the other side of the hill were the tattered remains of a few wings, paper and butterfly, but that was all.

Thorontur glanced down at the ruins of the lentaja and pursed his lips. "It was well that the dragons of old did not have those strange creatures as their allies."

Tillit shouldered his cannon and grinned. "Glad to be of service, and about that trade. . ."

I rolled my eyes before I walked over to meet Xander at the edge of the top. He reverted to his human form and studied my face. "Are you all right?"

I pursed my lips and glanced over my shoulder at where Sala had disappeared. "To be honest, the last god-sending was a little easier."

Xander wrapped his arms around me and pressed me against his chest. I appreciated the warmth of his strong body and his soft words. "Our task is nearly complete."

I sighed. "Yeah, just two more. . ."

"I am sorry I was not of more assistance in this adventure."

I snorted and pushed us apart so I could look up into his face. "Yeah, you were kind of sleeping on the job, weren't you?"

He smiled down at me. "If it is any consolation my dreams were full of you."

"In the mortal danger I was in?" I quipped.

He furrowed his brow as he looked past me at our friends. "The danger must have been great to change the mind of Thorontur."

I turned around and watched our friends-fae, human, and sus-congratulate one another on a battle well-won. A smile slipped onto my lips as Xander pressed a soft kiss against my forehead. "I am proud of you."

I looked up at him and gave a playful glare. "You'd better be. I'm the one who did all the heavy lifting this time."

He swept me into his arms and lifted me against his chest. "Then I shall do the lifting for the remainder of our time here."

I wrapped my arms around his neck and grinned. "Just like a lord to treat his woman like a lady."

We joined our friends in their congratulations, but soon left that area of devastation. Unfortunately, our path was as troublesome as the first time, but without the divine help. Halfway to the city we came upon our old friends, the werewolves. The beasts, twice as many as before, slunk from the shadows rather than leapt, but their eyes were still full of a strong hatred as they glared at the fae king.

Their leader, a husky wolf with a scar across his cheek, confronted Thorontur. "You played us for fools earlier, fae king, but now I've brought all my people."

FOREST OF THE DRAGON

Thorontur glanced at our group and smiled. "My friends, I am afraid I must force us to pause for just a moment while I manage them."

Mies shook his head. "Not just you." He drew out his sword and grinned at the wolves as some of them shrank back from the blade. "I'd like a little fun, too."

"I will help," Muffy offered.

"Don't leave Tillit out," our sus friend spoke up.

The lead werewolf chuckled. "You think you humans can handle my men?"

Darbat held his arms out on either side of him and conjured two spinning blades of wind. "I believe we can."

The werewolves blinked in bewilderment at his magic. That's all the time they had before we descended on them with all the fury of exhausted travelers eager to get home. A minute later the last werewolf, the leader, scooted away into the darkness.

I wrinkled my nose as I smelled the scent of wet dog. "Maybe I should've let you guys do all the work."

Tillit closed his bag of wonders and slung it over one shoulder before he rubbed his knuckles. "Their jaws are as thick as their skulls."

Thorontur mounted his steed and smiled at his friends. "I believe they will no longer bother my-" his gaze fell on Mies, "-*our* people again."

Mies climbed onto his horse and grinned. "Good. I never liked dogs."

We continued on our way, and soon the city of Metsan Keskella rose up before us. A cry went up from the guards on the walls as we approached, and Durion met us at the front gates.

"What happened?" he asked us.

Thorontur slipped down from his horse and walked over to his son. He grasped his upper arms and looked him in the eyes. "I have been such a fool."

Durion blinked at him. "Father?"

Thorontur turned and stepped back to stand by his son's side as he swept his arm over the human part of our group. "These humans showed a bravery I did not suspect they possessed, and a kindness that equals even your own." He glanced at his son and smiled. "We will have peace."

A smile brightened Durion's face as he patted his father on the shoulder. "I am glad to hear that."

Mies dismounted and strode up to Durion. "How's my daughter?"

"She is awake, as are the rest of your men," Durion assured him.

Mies grinned. "That's my girl. If you'll excuse me, gentlemen." He hurried off to see his little girl and his men.

Thorontur turned to the city and swept his eyes over the tall, thick walls. "I believe I have a better plan for protecting our people." He glanced at his son. "Arrange for everyone to meet before the palace. No one should be spared."

Durion arched an eyebrow. "What is it?"

Thorontur smiled at him and gave a wink. "You will see soon enough."

Durion furrowed his brow, but bowed his head and hurried to dispense with the orders. Xander and I walked up to the fae king, and a sly smile slipped onto the lips of my dragon lord. "I know you, King Thorontur. You have a secret."

Thorontur's eyes sparkled as they flickered to us. "We shall call it a 'hunch.'"

I winced and rubbed my derriere. "I'm going to call it saddle-sore."

"You are welcome to rest in the palace," he offered. "It will take some time to gather all my people."

We retired to our usual room where Darda drew out the chime box from her dress and set it gingerly on the table in the room. Xander furrowed his brow before he walked over and drew the bell from the box. He lifted the bell and looked on its edge.

"What's it read?" I asked from the bed.

He set the bell back in the box and shook his head. "There is nothing."

I wrinkled my nose. "That won't help us. Maybe we need to get out of here for it to tell us."

"Perhaps," he agreed.

I flopped backward and closed my eyes. "Wake me when Thorontur's fun starts."

My nap lasted two hours, and I was awoken for the gathering. We joined the fae king and our human friends, Vato included, before the large gates to the palace. Before us stood the thousands of Arbor fae that inhabited the city. Young and old, men and women, in a crowd that stretched left and right and down into the houses.

Thorontur stepped to the forefront of our group and raised his arms above his head. The whole kingdom quieted. "I am sure many of you heard that our god, Lord Luoja, returned, albeit briefly. He has gone again, but he has left a gift to us. This gift also comes with a great responsibility, and as keepers of the woods for the dragons of Alexandria, we have a duty to protect all who reside in the forest."

"Except werewolves. . ." I muttered.

"These humans-" Thorontur gestured to Mies and the others, "-have come to claim what they have earned after countless generations of penance, but they are in need of our protection. With the final gift of our god we must and will protect them so that both our peoples will thrive and once more live together in peace." A great cheer arose from the crowd. The guards banged the bottoms of their spears against the ground and nodded.

Thorontur smiled at his people with tears at his eyes. He raised his arms above him, and from the ground sprang a gentle forest of vines. The fae gasped and started back as they were surrounded by the jungle. Thorontur closed his eyes and furrowed his brow.

My eyes widened as I watched closed white flowers sprout from the vines. They parted and from them puffed the familiar mist that had hit Thorontur. The pollen wafted over the fae like a gentle wave. They started back as their hands glowed with their newfound energy.

"I give you your full powers like our ancestors of old held!" Thorontur announced.

A great jubilation arose from the crowd, along with more than one giant dirt pillar. Vines sprouted everywhere, but together they intertwined along the buildings and burst into full bloom. People laughed, cried, and danced among the explosion of greenery in an already-green city.

I leaned my head against Xander's side and smiled up at him. "Another happy ending."

Until our next, and final, adventure.

A note from Mac

Thank you for purchasing my book! Your support means a lot to me, and I'm grateful to have the opportunity to entertain you with my stories.

If you'd like to continue reading the series, or wonder what else I might have up my writer's sleeve, feel free to check out my website at *macflynn.com*, or contact me at mac@macflynn.com.

* * *

Want to get an email when the next book is released? Sign up for the Wolf Den, the online newsletter with a bite, at *eepurl.com/tm-vn*!

Continue the adventure

Now that you've finished the book, feel free to check out my website at **macflynn.com** for the rest of the exciting series.

Here's also a little sneak-peek at the next book:

Dreams of Dragons:

> It was dark. And cramped. And generally just damn uncomfortable
> I shifted and winced as a stack of quills poked me in the back. So much for this being a good hiding spot.
> A clatter of feet made me freeze. They paused. There came the sound of soft breathing.
> "Where'd she go?" a small voice asked.
> "I don't know, but she's gotta be here somewhere."
> Please don't open the door. I moved again and winced as I was again stabbed by the unrelenting quills. Please open the door.
> "What are you children doing in here?" a harsh voice snapped.
> "Run!"
> There was the clatter of feet and then silence. A heavy pair of boots stalked over to my hiding spot. I held my breath.
> The pair of doors flung open and a sharp face stared into mine. The face belonged to a man, the former adviser of the kingdom of Alexandria, to be precise. His eyes widened and he leapt back with a high-

pitched scream I didn't realize a man was capable of making.

I tumbled onto the hard floor and found myself on my back. Around me were dozens of long, tall shelves filled with all the knowledge of the kingdom of Alexandria passed down and painstakingly cataloged for future generations.

Also, one of its quill cupboards had been my hiding spot in a lively game of hide-and-seek.

Renner, the former adviser to Xander, glared at me. In his arms were a half dozen scrolls. The older gentleman had ditched his flowing blue robe with green hems for a plain gray robe with white hems.

He raised himself to his full, skinny height and looked down his thin nose at me. "What are you doing in here?"

I sat up and winced as my back popped. "Would you believe I was improving my mind?"

"I would not."

I stood and stretched my aching legs. "I wouldn't believe it, either."

A noise in the hall outside the doorway made me glance in that direction and forced Renner to half-turn around. "She's trapped, Darda! You have to save her!" insisted the small voice from before.

"Yeah! A mean man has her!" the other voice agreed.

"Has who?" Darda asked them.

Darda appeared in the doorway, and on each hand hung a small child. One was a boy of seven and the other a girl of five.

The girl pointed at Renner. "He has her!"

The boy's gaze fell on me and his face lit up with a smile. "Miriam! We found you!"

I jerked my thumb at Renner. "Actually, he found me first, so he wins."

Renner looked aghast at me. "You were using the sacred library as a game room?"

"No, as a hiding spot," I corrected him.

Renner's face turned an unsightly shade of red. Darda noticed and leaned down so she was closer to the height of the children. "Run along now. I must speak with Miriam."

Their faces fell. "Do we have to?" the boy asked.

"I want to stay with Miriam!" the girl whimpered.

"I think the chef has some cookies for you in the kitchen," Darda tempted them.

They didn't need a second invitation. The pair dropped her hands so fast that I think they snapped against Darda's sides. They bolted down the hall and their clattering soon faded away.

Renner boiled over like a cauldron left too long over a bonfire. "You dare use the library for your foolishness? You who is lady of this magnificent kingdom and Maiden to the great Xander?"

"It had the best hiding spots," I countered.

Darda hurried up to my side and faced Renner. "I believe what Miriam is trying to say is she meant no disrespect."

He snorted. "I dare say she did not! What is this library but the favorite place of her predecessor, the beloved Lady Catherine? Why not besmirch her memory for the sake of frivolous fun?"

I frowned. "I didn't mean any disrespect, especially not to Xander's mom. I was just trying to have fun with some of the castle kids."

Renner sneered at me. "Lady Catherine was capable of entertaining the children through reading the books, not abusing them."

"Sir Renner, I believe that is quite enough," Darda scolded him.

Renner's sneer dropped a little before he pushed past me and over to the quill cabinet. He knelt down and muttered a few words of which I only caught a handful. ". . .a shadow of My Lady. . ."

Darda looped her arm through mine and marched me out of the library. The smooth cobble stones were mercilessly pounded by her feet as she shook her head. "The insolence of that man! As though his own actions did not lose him the position of adviser! I will inform Xander of this outrage immediately."

"It's okay."

She whipped her head to me and furrowed her brow. "But he insulted you, Miriam! How can you be so forgiving over his unkind words?"

I smiled back at her. "Because I don't think I'm as much a lady as Xander's mom. I mean-" we stopped in the hall and I gestured to the head of a statue in an alcove. The bust was of the beautiful Lady Cate decked out in a tiara and with a bright, gentle smile on her face. "-there's about a dozen of these busts around the place, and that's just by this one artist. That doesn't include the portraits, the life-size statues, and even a dinner plate featuring her face."

"And there is the fountain statue in one of the courtyards," she reminded me.

I snorted. "See? It's a tough act to follow."

"But you saved the world many times," she countered.

"Yeah, but it's really hard to be patted on the back when most people didn't even know there was world-wide peril," I pointed out.

Darda pursed her lips as she studied me. "I for one believe you are as much a lady as Lady Cate. Well-" her eyes flickered down to my comfortable attire of jeans and a t-shirt, "-that is, in actions, if not in dress and manners."

I snorted. "Thanks. That makes me feel better."

"Are you ill?" a voice spoke up. We glanced down the hall to see Xander approach us.

I rubbed my back. "No, but I could use a massage after hiding in that cabinet."

Xander stopped before us and blinked at me. "Hiding in a cabinet? What was the occasion?"

"A game of hide-and-seek where it was two against one," I told him.

A smile slipped onto his lips. "Did you win?"

I stretched my back and winced as the lower part popped. "Yes and no."

Xander chuckled as he set his hand on my lower back just below the ache. "A massage would do you well," he mused as he led me down the hall.

"Might I offer my services?" Darda spoke up.

Xander looked over his shoulder and winked at her. "I believe I will handle this duty, Darda."

She straightened and her face blushed. "Oh! Yes! Of course!"

I glanced up at his mischievous smile as he led me in the general direction of our bedroom. "You're supposed to relax tight muscles, not tighten them further."

He chuckled. "I promise you will be very relaxed afterward."

We stepped through an archway and I tripped over a change in the flooring. Xander caught me before I fell and I got a good look at the floor. The smooth cobblestones of the hall changed to long wood planks. I raised my head and my face fell.

We stood in the lobby of the Mallus Library. The caretaker himself, Crates, stood near the wide opening to the countless bookcases. His hands were clasped behind his back and his expression was as dark as the books that lay in darkness. The whole place was illuminated only by a few candles that hung on holders beside the bookcases.

I straightened and frowned. "Come on. We didn't even go through a door that time."

Crates took a step forward and pursed his lips. "I apologize for the rough entrance, but we have much to discuss."

"You mean the two missing gods?" I guessed. He gave a nod. "Are they really that much trouble? I mean, it's been three months since our last fight and the world hasn't ended."

"The world continues to hang in the balance, though I have watched you from afar and must congratulate you on your many amazing feats," he complimented us.

"We couldn't have done it last time without our friends," I pointed out.

The corners of his lips twitched upward. "Yes. Like nature attracts like nature, and around you have amassed a wealth of such special people. However-" his face fell as he looked from Xander to me., "-the final two gods have made themselves known to me, and I feel I must warn you about one of them."

"How do they 'make themselves known to you?'" I asked him.

He swept his hand over the countless books at his back. "The vast knowledge of this library, and the location of your own battles, has allowed me to ascertain the identities of the remaining gods. Though I am bound to keep most information from you, I can warn you that one of those ethereal creatures is by far the most dangerous of any that remained in your world."

Xander arched an eyebrow. "In what way?"

Crates shook his head. "I cannot give you any specifics other than to say this creature will test your bonds-and even your sanity-like no other. You must keep your faith in one another and hold tight to what you know is the truth."

My face fell. "That's it? That's your 'specifics?' I get better advice from a fortune cookie."

His unblinking eyes fell on me and I shivered as I felt a cold chill sink into me. "You will tested the worst of all, Miriam, so I will give you further advice: keep the chime to yourself and do not give it over to anyone."

I arched an eyebrow. "Not even Xander?"

"No one."

I held up my hands in front of me. "All right, no one. Is there anything else you can tell us about this unspeakable evil?"

"You will know all too soon." He raised his hand and snapped his fingers. Invisible hands pressed against our fronts and pushed us backward toward the archway at our backs. Our last view of the old caretaker was of him raising his hand in farewell to us. "Good luck, my friends. You will need all you can find."

We were pushed through the archway and the view of the library in front of us vanished like a card in the hand of a magician. I looked up at Xander and frowned. "This sounds like fun."

He pursed his lips and gave a nod. "Yes. We have our hardest fights before us."

A thought hit me and I threw up my arms. "Crates didn't even tell us where these last two gods were!"

A horn blew loud and clear through the castle. Xander stiffened and whipped his head around so he looked at the front of the building that faced the lake. "What? What is it?" I asked him.

His eyebrows crashed down. "Trouble."

Other series by Mac Flynn

Contemporary Romance
Being Me
Billionaire Seeking Bride
The Family Business
Loving Places
PALE Series
Trapped In Temptation

Demon Romance
Ensnare: The Librarian's Lover
Ensnare: The Passenger's Pleasure
Incubus Among Us
Lovers of Legend
Office Duties
Sensual Sweets
Unnatural Lover

Dragon Romance
Blood Dragon
Dragon Bound
Maiden to the Dragon

Ghost Romance
Phantom Touch

Vampire Romance
Blood Thief
Blood Treasure
Vampire Dead-tective
Vampire Soul

Urban Fantasy Romance
Death Touched

Werewolf Romance
Alpha Blood
Alpha Mated
Beast Billionaire
By My Light
Desired By the Wolf
Falling For A Wolf
Garden of the Wolf
Highland Moon
In the Loup
Luna Proxy
Marked By the Wolf
Moon Chosen
The Moon and the Stars
Moon Lovers
Oracle of Spirits
Scent of Scotland: Lord of Moray
Shadow of the Moon
Sweet & Sour
Wolf Lake

Manufactured by Amazon.ca
Bolton, ON